eGo

A Dot-com Bubble Story

by Ed SJC Park

Copyright © 2012 by Ed Park

All rights reserved.

No part of this book may be reproduced in any form or by any electronic or mechanical means including information storage and retrieval systems, without permission in writing from the author. The only exception is by a reviewer, who may quote short excerpts in a review.

Printed in the United States of America

First Printing: 2012

ISBN 978-1-105-87089-7

Dedicated to

Beverly B, Debbie, Laura, Annie, Erin, Julio O, Sebastian M, Brad D, and the 1990's

Table of Contents

CHAPTER 1: HAVING A FUTURE 5
CHAPTER 2: BACK TO THE BAY 16
CHAPTER 3: IRONICISM 21
CHAPTER 4: LUST 37
CHAPTER 5: TWEAKER 49
CHAPTER 6: ENVY, PRIDE, AND WRATH 57
CHAPTER 7: PLAYING BY THE RULES 67
CHAPTER 8: DELUSION 75
CHAPTER 9: MURDER 99
CHAPTER 10: GLUTTONY AND SLOTH 109
CHAPTER 11: GREED AND ACEDIA 134

Chapter 1: Having a Future

After graduating from Stanford in 1994, I found myself unemployed. My smarter classmates were all going off to grad school. I moved to San Francisco in the midst of California's big, fat recession. I languished there from one temp job to another. My specialty had become data entry. Having spent a summer interning at the business school entering data, it was my only real job skill. My Economics major was about as impressive to employers as was my interest in writing novels. I did actually land one nice job, but it was only temporary. In 1998 and almost traumatized by four years of disappointment and failure, a friend of mine moved to Reno and suggested that I move there in search of work. Nevada's economy was doing much better than California's. Reno opened a major casino, the Silver Legacy in 1995 and people were still gambling.

I always considered myself a rather intelligent person. My high SAT scores could attest to that, but one of my coworkers once told me that I was too smart for my own good. I never really understood that observation until I thought about it more for several years. I think he meant that I tend to over-analyze and over-think things. You can be "book smart" and have utterly no common sense or savvy. In college and through much of schooling, you are taught that the one who gets the highest grades is the best student. It's as simple as that. If you want to be the best student, you get the highest grades, and then the valedictorian and cum laude's are like the gods of academia. Well, in the real world, the best employee is not the one who has the best marks in college and gets the job done fastest or best. Actually, even in school, you can be the best student and also the worst kid in school as far as popularity. However, in the real world, the work world, you can be the best worker and still get fired or passed up for promotion to worse employees who happen to be more popular. This is the one big lesson you just don't learn in school. Another big lesson is that you don't have to do your job perfectly. In school, you cross all your t's and dot all your i's and if you hand in a research paper, it has to be perfect: no sloppy reasoning, analysis, or research methodologies. In the real world, it's all about what works well enough, and time and price are critical factors. There's a reason there are auto repair shops. You're not buying perfect products.

Fact is, I was a really good, hardworking, fast, efficient, and smart worker who could always analyze the job and come up with a hundred better ways of doing everything, but in reality, I was just some obnoxious, annoying, nerd who wasn't popular and never got hired or promoted. Fitting in is a big part of career success and getting along with your boss is even bigger. I never much cared for most of my bosses who tended to be less educated, less intellectual, and less idea-oriented. Of course, this is all hindsight. Back then, I just blamed everyone and everything for my misfortunes.

My life, however, turned around when I moved to Reno. I started out taking temp jobs like in San Francisco, but just a few months in, I interviewed for a full-time permanent job with a battery supply company called "Full Charge." At first, I just imagined that they sold car batteries, but as it turned out, they sold all types of batteries mostly for small electronic devices and cell phones. They considered themselves a high-tech company, but I considered them a simple catalogue supply business. They were based in San Francisco interestingly, but they were moving their entire operations to Reno. They would train me for a month in San Francisco and then I'd work in their Reno office.

Full Charge set up their interviews at two locations. The first was their new office and warehouse in Northwest Reno. I had just moved to Reno, so it was an all new area for me, sparsely populated. People in Reno today would not recognize the old Northwest Reno. There were only two apartment complexes out there compared to today where they dominate the entire area. There wasn't even any bus service out there. Yeah, I had become so broke I was living in a weekly motel and couldn't afford a car. So I took a taxi out there.

There was a front office attached to a large warehouse. I sat in the lobby area, and I immediately noticed a very busty, hot blonde sitting there too. Naturally, I started small talk with her. She was a local looking for one of their customer service rep jobs. I felt sort of stupid telling her I was looking into their data entry jobs. I probably would have felt even worse if she had seen me taking a cab. She walked in for the interview. Later on, I was interviewed by an old guy named Terri. He was a nerdy type who seemed distracted and a bit confused. He wore bifocals and whenever he looked at me, he'd lower his head so he could see over the top part of the bifocals.

"Stanford?" His eyes widened. "You were only there three years though."

"Yeah, I took summer classes and graduated a year early."

"Impressive!"

I didn't put down my GPA or anything. I actually graduated with a B-average. I wasn't a genius who graduated in three years because I was so smart. I was just tired of Economics and studying and wanted to get out of there as quickly as possible. I took easy elective classes over the summer like literature, philosophy, color, and acting.

"Temp agencies," he noted.

I wanted to apologize. I knew what he was thinking. Why would a guy who graduated from Stanford in three years spend the next four years temping, and not temping like accounting or finance, but temping data entry at $8/hour?

"The economy's been tough. I've just taken work where I can find it."

"Yeah, sure, sure. Don't you think you can find something better? Something in a management training program, financial analysis, an entry level financial position maybe."

"I put out resumes all over the Bay area. Just haven't made much progress there. I'd love to take a management training program, some entry level financial analysis." Honestly, I'm not sure why, but I never really did try. I was offered a Wall Street stock broker job, but they told me I'd have to pass some exam, and the last thing I wanted to do was spend any more time studying. I guess I needed a mental break. Stuffing four years of college into three years had pushed me a bit much, and I almost had a nervous breakdown my last year in college. I was lost. I thought I wanted to become this big corporate business tycoon and make loads of money, but I couldn't stand accounting and finance. I couldn't stand rules and memorizing rules and following rules. I spent most of my time focusing on my literature, philosophy, and psychology classes. They fascinated me a billion times more. They told me about the important things in life: people, relationships, behavior, thoughts, existence, life, reality. Finance and Accounting told me nothing about these things. It was all a bunch of bullshit rules to memorize, and at the end of the day, all you had was a better understanding of the rules. You didn't know anything more about life, your life, yourself, others, reality, people, how people work, how you work, think. I wanted to know all that shit. I didn't want to know how to balance a fucking balance sheet or amortize a stupid loan. I thought about it a lot. Maybe it was my mother who was so psychotic it made me wonder what life was all about and why people went crazy. She also had all these stupid rules that made no sense, and she was never consistent about them, and she often punished me out of anger more than anything else. Naturally, I just grew up to despise rules and those who enforced them. Was this why I flunked out of Finance and Accounting?

I studied Economics, because I thought it would teach me about the real world, real economies, real countries, economic development, policies. All I studied were endless fucking calculus formulas and graphs. It was beyond abstract. In one class, we spent the entire class breaking apart a foreign exchange interest formula and then putting it all back together again. That was it. I felt like a fucking computer could do it. Is this why I was put on this planet? To be a fucking computer, to eat numbers, pass them through an intestinal algorithm, and shit them out my ass? You know there are infinite points in a curve, no, infinite fucking boredom. I wanted meaning and substance. I wanted what you got when you put all the boring infinite points together. All I had was number crunching. Then I guess the most horrific irony of all was how I spent the next four years doing nothing but number crunching as a data entry clerk bored out of my fucking mind, but not being paid $50K a year but $8 fucking dollars an hour. When coworkers asked me if I went to college, I used to tell them Stanford, and they'd look at me real funny. I quickly learned to tell them community college. Not one of them was a college grad.

Terri came across as a warm and caring guy. And when he told me that he felt I was over-qualified for a data entry clerk, he did it like he really cared about me, not like he worried that I'd get bored and quit after a few weeks and cost the company money in training hours.

"Well, I've done it the last four years. I can handle it. When the economy turns around, I might look for something else, but I think I've gotten pretty good at it. I type 70 words per minute and ten key 15,000." I was really fast, too fast. Temp agencies actually didn't like me, because they'd send me out to do a four week assignment, and I'd be done in less than two weeks. They didn't give a fuck if I was fast and efficient for the client. They lost over two weeks of income. They fucking hated me. They'd send me out on one day assignments, and I'd be done by lunch. They fucking hated me and gave better assignments to slower idiots with GED's.

Most people would go nuts keying in a string of numbers in a dozen different fields all day long, but I was able to allow my mind to wander, to think, imagine, fantasize, day dream. I thought up all sorts of things from new novels to screenplays and remembering moments from my past in San Francisco, college, high school. I'd think about daily news, politics, current affairs, scandals, celebrities, sports. My mind was constantly on. I couldn't stop thinking. The only time I ever stop thinking is when I'm sleeping or drunk, but even then, fuck I think in my dreams, I think about stupid stuff when I'm drunk. I listen to songs like, "Bad Moon Rising," and I'm thinking, fucking-a, they're singing about the end of the world.

"Well, we are a fast growing company, and there will be opportunities for advancement. Okay, I think this may work. We're the kind of company that strives to be the best, and we hire the best too. Probably all of our employees are overqualified. We're a very ambitious, fast-paced company. Do you think you can handle that?"

"I think I'd be bored otherwise."

He smiled.

"Okay, there's a second set of interviews where you'll get to meet the company's owner and two other people. It's at the Reno Hilton, not the Flamingo Hilton downtown, but the one by the airport. I'll set up an interview for you for tomorrow."

I wasn't sure why there were two interviews for a stupid data entry position, but I wasn't complaining. Terri seemed to genuinely like me and probably would put in a good word for me. The next day, I went to the Hilton. It was a bit intimidating. There were two guys and a very attractive woman. They were all tall and wore black suits. They looked very professional. Terri looked more casual and warm. These guys looked like they worked on the Death Star alongside Darth Vader. It was also considerably darker in the convention room which also created a more formal, serious air.

The owner, Sam Thompson, came across as a bit disinterested and aloof. He kept leaning back and resting his arms behind his head. I read a book on body language in college, and this was a typical exaggerated display of dominance. Basically, he was exposing his armpits, airing them out, tainting the air with his body odor, marking his territory. Also, by leaning back, he was looking down at me. You look down on someone when you are taller which often means older. I wasn't impressed by him, but he was impressed by the fact that I had graduated from Stanford. He never mentioned anything about me being overqualified or anything. It was a short interview, and I went to the next guy.

The next guy was Stephen. He was not only tall but muscular and huge. He looked like a bouncer. He came across as a lot warmer and nicer. He was one of those big, soft, cuddly bears like John Wilkos on *Jerry Springer*. It was easy talking to him, and he too didn't mention anything about me being over-qualified. In fact, as it turned out, he used to play college baseball and asked me about Stanford's team. Unfortunately, I didn't know much about them, but I told him I liked the San Francisco Giants. He asked me if I ever went to a game, and I said I didn't. I felt like I was trying to bullshit him, but he wasn't the kind of guy to call me on it. He just seemed to give me the benefit of the doubt. He gave me a handshake and I thought he'd tear my hand off, but surprising it was an easy, soft shake. I was feeling a lot better now.

My last interview was with Marla. Marla was gorgeous. I instantly started fantasizing about hitting on her at work and perhaps even dating her. I kept staring at the pendant on her necklace that hung a few inches between each of her nipples. For whatever reason, the interview with Marla became more of personal interview than a professional one.

"So what brings you to Reno?"

"Work," I smiled. She smiled. "I mean, Reno has a better job market than California. I love San Francisco. I left my heart in San Francisco, but I'd rather be employed in Reno than homeless in San Francisco."

"There's a lot of homeless in San Francisco."

"Yes, I'd have a lot of company." Her smile was so beautiful.

"I know, you have to be careful walking around or else you'll accidentally step on one."

"And then, you'd have to give him change right?"

She laughed.

"Unless he's asleep, I'd just keep walking."

She laughed more. "I love San Francisco too, but my husband lives here and his whole family too. I'm from the Midwest."

"Oh, what state?"

"Wisconsin."

"Oh, you don't have a Wisconsin accent."

"Oh, don't cha know."

"Yah, yah," I replied.

We both laughed. *Fargo* had come out a couple years ago. I'm not one of those annoying types to imitate any weird accent to come out of a movie like Yoda, Jack Nicholson, Clint Eastwood, Robert DeNiro, John Wayne, Harold Lloyd. But I did do the whole *Fargo* thing, because it's funny.

"That's North Dakota. Do they speak like that in Wisconsin?" I asked.

"I have relatives who speak like that. Sometimes you can catch me. Where are you from?"

"I'm from Washington, the state. We don't have an accent. I'm sure we do, but I guess everyone thinks wherever they're from, they're the ones without an accent."

"Can't really tell a Washington accent. Maybe a Nirvana accent, nasally, whiney?"

I feigned injury. "Nasal and whiney? Is that how I sound?"

"I'm just kidding." She glanced my resume.

"So you're not from San Francisco?" I asked.

"No, I got hired here a month ago."

"Oh, and you're doing interviews?"

"Yeah, crazy. I'm like the company spokesperson too, I know everything about it right?"

In my mind, I was thinking of saying, "*You could be the company spokesmodel,*" but I thought twice and imagined it was a bit much.

"How do you like working here so far?" I asked instead.

"It's very fast-paced. It's chaotic, but fun. I enjoy the challenges. Stanford is a really good school."

"Oh no, it's Stanford City Community College." She looked at me. "I'm just kidding. Yeah, it's a great school. Last year, the job board was filled with companies looking to hire: Cisco, eBay, Bank of America, Apple, Hewlett Packard, Intel, Wells Fargo, Charles Schwab. Then the year I graduated, nothing, nada. Well, there was Macy's and Ghirardelli's."

"The chocolate?"

"Yeah. I think it's overrated. I prefer real Belgian."

"Love Belgian chocolate."

"I actually love to write. I spent a lot of time in college just writing."

"Non-fiction? Fiction?"

"Fiction."

"Like what kind? Mysteries?"

"Weird fiction."

"Weird fiction?"

"Surrealist fiction. My writing professor never really understood it. Just weird stuff, not science fiction, I guess maybe Edgar Allan Poe would be a close comparison, but it wasn't so much about hauntings and dark stuff, just weird. It's hard to explain, like a ten year-old with a 40 year-old's mind, thinking and talking like a 40 year-old but living a ten year-old's life."

"Wow, that sounds really interesting."

"Yeah, just stuff you don't expect, feelings, moods. I took a class in German Romantic Literature, and it's not romantic as in romance novels, but the Romantic Period, and it's all about the uncanny, the eerie, the unorthodox."

"Have you published anything yet?"

"No, not yet, but one day."

"Well, when you do, you'll have to sign my copy."

"I will."

"Well, you're certainly qualified, maybe over-qualified for the position, but there are opportunities to advance. I enjoyed talking with you Bill."

"Yeah, me too." We made eye contact for a moment. I was sure she was flirting with me, but maybe I was just deranged.

"We'll give you a call soon."

"If I do make it to San Francisco, I'll have to show you around. There's a lot of great places tourists miss."

"Yeah," she smiled, "that sounds great. I'll look forward to it."

We shook hands, and perhaps it lasted a smidge too long, but I didn't care. I felt I had the job in the bag. It was probably very inappropriate and unprofessional of me, and with any other woman, probably also offensive and insulting, but she seemed to enjoy the casual atmosphere, probably a break from all the other interviewees who were probably boring, tense, and nervous. Near the end, I was almost tempted to ask her for her personal phone number and take her out to dinner.

It only occurred to me then that interviewing was all about making a personal connection, and it was just like a first date. I mean, you do have the factual stuff, your qualifications, your stats, your past history, but ultimately, you got hired on your ability to connect with the person. I failed a lot of interviews in San Francisco probably because I hid behind my resume, stuck with the facts, never relaxed and opened up and created any opportunity for a personal connection. If only every interviewer was a stunning, hot babe with perky tits.

As I was waiting for the bus outside the Reno Hilton, looking at the mountains in the distance, I considered this a whole new chapter in my life. I had been struggling badly the last four years. It was odd how moving ahead in Reno meant going back over those mountains back to San Francisco for a month. This would be my first full time job out of college. If I stuck with this company, I could possibly make a career of it. I could save up enough money to get a car, an apartment, become a normal person again, and then return to San Francisco some day. Of course, I'd always have my writing ambition on the side, but things would be easier now. I'd actually have the money and security now to enjoy life.

The following day, Terri called me and offered me the job. He told me that on Sunday evening, he was driving down to San Francisco and surprisingly offered me a ride. Since I was living in a weekly motel out of my duffel bag, it didn't take me long to get all my stuff ready and move. I took a taxi down to his house, and he told me it was in a gated community at Lake Stanley and to tell the guard I was here for Terri. Terri lived in a really nice, big contemporary house. I was really surprised actually. I saw him in an old, ugly conventional, suburban house with one of those ugly swinging, porch benches. He seemed too old and plain for this house which seemed fit for some famous actor, recording artist, or Wall Street yuppie. Then Terri surprised me again by telling me that I could rent out a room in his house. It was tempting, but ultimately, I liked my privacy. He had two young kids, and I didn't want to have to deal with them going to the refrigerator or using the laundry. I figured he'd probably try to get me to babysit them too. Then again, if I was living in the house, why would he need a babysitter? The house was also considerably far from any bus stop. I could hitch a ride with Terri to work and back, but Terri told me that he liked to start work early and often stayed late. I didn't like that kind of dependence and worse getting up so early. I kindly declined the offer but said I'd keep it in mind. It was a bit odd how generous and open he was.

On the way to San Francisco, I saw a falling star, and accordingly made a wish. I wished that I would someday get a novel published. I never imagined that novel would be about my experience at this company.

Chapter 2: Back to the Bay

The warehouse and office of Full Charge was not in San Francisco but South San Francisco, a considerable distance from downtown San Francisco. It was situated near the bay and there would often be an eerie fog meandering around the streets. You could see planes cross the bay as they landed at SFO. It was an electrifying and exciting month. I met a whole new cast of characters, quite a few young customer service and data entry clerks as well as older supervisors and managers. I quickly learned that Sam was one of those crazy bosses. He was mercurial, ill-tempered, demanding, detail-oriented, obsessive, and moody. The worst thing you could do there was piss off the customer with some stupid mistake. The customer was king. Everyone got the talk. A few weeks in, even I got the talk. It was a humiliating experience. It was somewhere between a kid being scolded for drawing with a crayon on the wall and a dog having its face smeared in its own pee on the floor.

"Were you taught how to run the invoice printer?" Sam asked rhetorically.

"Yeah. I was taught how to do it." There was pressure building under my eyes. It wasn't to cry. For whatever reason, when I feel embarrassed or humiliated, I feel pressure building right under my eyes almost like a sinus, allergic reaction. Everything I ever built as a kid, a big Lego castle, a model ship with sails and rigging and all, my mother would smash just for laughs. I'd get the same swelling pressure under my eyes, not to cry, just humiliation and perhaps rage. I quickly learned not to construct anything big. Unfortunately, I couldn't make my plants stop growing, and my mother one day in the winter threw them all out and within a few days, insects had eaten them all. Sometimes I wondered if this was why I started so many projects and novels and never finished any of them.

"So you know how to do it. You've been here two weeks. You know how it works."

"Yeah. I've run the invoices before. I just wasn't paying attention." I tried to be calm, docile, not overly subservient.

"It costs money. It's wasteful to screw up so many labels. What's worse is not paying attention. You have to pay closer attention." Back then, they were still using some old dot-matrix printer to print out invoices. You had to line it up perfectly, or you'd get hundreds of fucked up invoices with printing all in the wrong boxes and lines. I had checked the first few invoices, but I swear to God the printer would jump a line regularly. I wasn't going to fucking stand there all day watching the invoice printer.

"If you're not paying attention to the invoices, what else are you not paying attention to? Orders? Quantities? Product numbers? Addresses? You see what I mean. You think we're here talking about invoices, but what I'm talking about is more than just stupid invoices. I'm talking about paying attention. I don't like sloppy workers. I fire sloppy workers. They can go work at McDonalds. How can you fuck up a burger and fries? And even if you do, who the fuck cares?"

I was thinking to myself, I'd fucking care. And you can fuck up burgers and fries. You can burn the burger or undercook it and make someone sick. You can put too much salt on the fries or not enough. Seriously, this guy needed to work on his metaphors.

"I don't run a sloppy company here. I don't want sloppy workers. I expect more from you. This will never happen again, and I'm not just talking about invoices right?"

"Yeah. I understand. I'll pay attention to everything I do. I'll be a lot more – I'll be more focused."

Sam looked over at his computer. He was distracted by something. I stood there like a tool. I wondered if that was it. It wasn't so bad. I heard that he could make people cry. I just felt stupid and humiliated. I never got told off like this since, I don't know, elementary school by a teacher, or constantly by my mother all my fucking life. It was embarrassing. It made me mad. It didn't make me feel motivated, that I would run out there and step up my game and do a better job. He was feeding us all this bullshit about how this was an innovative, cutting edge company, that he wanted the best of the best, yet it seemed like he just wanted brain-dead automatons incapable of creative thought, just scared out of their mind of making petty mistakes and being told off. He was cultivating an unhealthy atmosphere of fear and paranoia. Studies have shown if you want people to do something mundane efficiently, you can use simple carrots and sticks like money and chewing them out. But if you want people to do something innovative and thoughtful, money and degradation makes them worse. They need coaching and autonomy.

He looked at me oddly. "You can go back to work. That's what I'm paying you for."

In my mind, I let loose. "*You fucking dumb shit asshole moron idiot. You fucking hypocritical asswipe dehumanizing tool. Fuck you, and fuck your 'say no to sloppy' fucked up company, and I could care less if I get fired from this freak show, you fuckity fuck fuck fuck! Cunt face!!!!*"

I was just imaging Sam was one of those asshole bosses who would say things like, "I'm not paying you to think, I'm paying you print invoices!"

And I'd be like, "I'm not sure I understand."

And he'd be like, "Understand what? Your job is printing invoices. Stop thinking and just print invoices! How is that hard to understand?"

"Invoices? I, I don't get it. I'm printing invoices? I wasn't aware of that."

"What are you a fucking idiot? What the hell do you think you were printing?"

"I don't know. I'm confused. The printing, what's that?"

"What? What do you mean what is that? Your job is printing invoices."

"The printer thing. It's printing the invoice thing? The printer is printing the invoices, right?"

"Yes, Jesus, what is wrong with you? Are you a fucking moron? You are printing invoices! Do you need a fucking diagram?"

"Um, sure. Maybe that would clear things up, a diagram. See, you told me my job was not to think, so I'm like not fucking thinking, see how hard that makes things? I'm pretty fucking sure part of my job is thinking or else I wouldn't know what the fuck I was doing. Maybe your job is to start fucking thinking and quit telling everyone else to stop thinking, because apparently, you have no fucking idea what would happen if everyone stopped thinking."

One of the senior data entry clerks, Maude gave me a sympathetic look.

"It wasn't that bad," I told her.

"Don't worry about it. Just don't take it personally. That's how he operates. He puts fire under your heels. Sometimes it can be motivating, other times it can have the opposite effect. Just brush it off. I think you're doing a great job, and sooner or later, he'll figure that out and give you a break."

I hoped he would break his ass on the snow in Reno that fuck bag. Maude's intention was the best, but she sort of made me want to cry by being so sympathetic. She needed to shut the fuck up too.

The more I got to know the existing employees there, the more I started noticing cracks in the façade. Maude told me about how many promises he had broken. His original plan was to move most of his staff to Reno, but the closer they got to the moving date, the more they realized that he had no such intention. Maude already knew that her days were numbered. She had looked for a house in Reno, but a few days ago, Sam had told her that he wouldn't take her. In the month that I was there, I expected them to get rid of a few Reno folks who just couldn't cut it, but it was completely the opposite. Sam was firing his San Francisco staff left and right, people who had built the company with him from the ground up. He fired his graphic artist. He fired customer service reps. He fired an accountant. He fired the Marketing Director. People were dropping like flies. At this rate, it seemed, there would only be a handful of San Francisco people moving to Reno. He was basically getting all the Reno folks trained to replace almost his entire staff: Marketing, Accounting, Customer Service Reps, Data Entry, Warehouse, Sales, almost everyone.

In the meantime, I was having the time of my life hanging out with the Customer Service and Data Entry staff in what spare time we had. We had parties at our hotel rooms and one memorable party at a house near the beach where I was taught how to Salsa. I remember lunch time and the roach coach that came by. They had everything: candy, chips, donuts, sandwiches, soups, bagels, sodas. I could easily blow $10 on lunch, stuffing my face with a donut, sandwich, chips, and candy in one sitting. I probably gained a few pounds in San Francisco. But time flew fast. Our last weekend there, we all went to the city and partied. I hung out with one of the warehouse guys, and he got his first tattoo, well, at least the start of it. He passed out.

One night, we were cruising around, and he wasn't even drunk, and he just had a craving for donuts, and he saw this cop car in a parking lot, and I begged him not to. I told him, he'd get arrested or something. I don't think he was that smart. He was kind of simple-minded. He had some good ideas for the warehouse and showed me his set up plans for Reno, but I don't think he realized the full implications of what he was doing. But there was not an ounce of sarcasm in his voice when he asked the cop where the closest donut shop was. The cop didn't act like he was offended or anything and actually knew where the closest donut shop was. I couldn't stop laughing all the way to the donut shop.

I hadn't even planned on how to get home. I just assumed I could catch a ride with one of the Reno folks, but I didn't really know them that well. I thought about going with Marla, but I just never got around to talking to her about it. On Friday, realizing that my options had all ran out, I called Southwest Airlines from a payphone at the hotel and booked my return trip to Reno. The party was over.

Chapter 3: Ironicism

Back in Reno, I took a taxi a couple times and then arranged to get a ride from coworkers. It was a whole new atmosphere in Reno. We kept on hiring new people, and Mr. Thompson was getting more and more temperamental. People kept flying out the door, and it was creating an increasingly frenetic, paranoid atmosphere. I think Mr. Thompson was only in genocidal mode in San Francisco, but when he was like training all these senior level people from Reno, they must have been thinking, wow, Mr. Thompson fires people for smelling up the restroom, I guess back in Reno, I can fire people for just as trivial shit.

Back in San Francisco, Sam had made some really motivational speeches about working your ass off for something you believed in, and creating a world-class company with the highest standards of excellence. He actually made me feel like what I was doing was important. As a temp, no one ever made me feel like my job was important. It was often shit nobody else in the office wanted to do. They gave you a quick tour of the office, restrooms, break room, and then sat you down and told you what to do. Only one boss ever took me aside and talked to me like a human, asked me about my past and my future ambitions. I thought he was kind of a hippie for doing that, but I will never forget that. He made me feel like a human, not "*just a temp.*"

Mr. Thompson told everyone to read the book, *Principle Centered Leadership* by Stephen Covey. It was funny, because if anyone needed to read that book and follow its message, it was Sam. It was like the Pope telling everyone to read *Thus Spoke Zarathustra*. For whatever reasons, probably something in my childhood, I fed off the crazy. I can't stand static, secure environments. They bore me. I'm always watching what I'm saying or doing, thinking everyone is watching or judging me. There's a standard, and everyone has to fit that standard. It's all about fitting in and following the fucking rules. It's all about thriving to be perfectly mediocre. I thrived off the chaos, the fears, the traumas, the change, the constant change and growth. I was thriving for greatness or bust. We had two new people each week and fired one person. As one coworker liked to say, with Mr. Thompson, it's two steps forward, one step back.

One of the first people to go was the Data Entry Manager. I could never figure out why. In one particularly twisted scenario Marla somehow felt threatened by him, although, in San Francisco they seemed to be buddies. That's how working here made you feel. You just can't trust anyone. With people getting axed left and right, you just didn't know who your enemy was and you made strategic alliances with whomever you felt was on Mr. Thompson's good side. But then again, you just never knew, because that person could easily fall out of favor with Mr. Thompson and get axed. I decided from the beginning that the closer I got to Mr. Thompson, the higher chance for either promotion or death. I was happy just where I was. Meanwhile, Marla was working her way up the ladder and increasingly spending more time with Mr. Thompson.

At the same time, with no Data Entry Manager, I was promoted to Lead Data Processor, and I pretty much took on all the tasks of the manager. We were a good team, and I tried to shelter my staff from all the turbulence and drama in the office. I was proud to claim that Mr. Thompson never fired any of my staff. Unfortunately, I couldn't say the same for myself. I couldn't help but follow Sam's management style and axe people when they didn't hit the production quota. In my case, however, it was different, because we hired a lot of temp workers, and it was simply natural that we would come across someone who just wasn't up to par.

I probably should have realized this in hindsight, but my popularity was rising, and it was probably more a function of my rising status in the company. This was the first time in my life I was in charge of anyone, and when they promoted me to supervisor, I was a fish-out-of-water, but like all novices, I simply threw all my time and energy at the problem and hoped for the best.

I had never been in charge of anyone all my life. I was a rebel. I was all about breaking rules not following them. I was the kid at the back of the class daydreaming or making fun of the topic or teacher. I was fighting the system, the institution, the establishment, the man. I made fun of Mr. Thompson behind his back. I was one of those cool bosses, one of the guys. Only later, I'd realize that this was just one type of dysfunctional leader. I wasn't one of the guys. This is like a mom trying to be her daughter's best friend. I had the power to promote or fire everyone. They were being friendly with me, because they didn't want to get fired, not because I was a charming, funny, cool, rebellious guy.

But it was odd, that like a self-fulfilling prophecy, I became charming, funny, and cool. I joked around with them all and kept them cheery and laughing amidst all the chaos and confusion. Sometimes we had to put in 70 hour weeks, and at the end of the day when it was dark outside and everyone was getting fatigued, I'd break up the tension with jokes or just act crazy.

"Mr. Thompson sometimes reminds me of King Lear," I offered once.

"Who?" Janice asked.

I had already figured out by now to tone down my academic language and avoid terms like, "extrapolate" "obviate" "supplant" "preclude" "integral" "therefore." One data entry clerk told me to speak English once. It's funny, but everyone in Reno seems to like the term "intrical" which doesn't exist. Some bizarre hybrid of "integral" and "intricate." I created a Reno dictionary and grammar guideline and made fun of people in Reno.

The Reno Manual of Style

Mix "ex-" with "at-" and "acc-" or "es"

- extenuate becomes attenuate
- accessory becomes excessory
- ambidextrous becomes ambidestrous

- exceptional becomes acceptional
- accentuate becomes excentuate
- accessorize becomes excessorize

Replace "in-" with "un-"

- infrequent becomes unfrequent
- insurmountable becomes unsurmountable

If there is a word ending with "-ic" you can turn it into a verb or noun by replacing it with "-ify" or "-icize"

- generic becomes genericism or genericize
- dynamic becomes dynamicism or dynamicize
- eccentric becomes eccentricism or eccentricize

The Extraneous Vowel Rule: Add vowels to increase the number of syllables in a word

- expedite becomes expediate
- comparable becomes comparitable

Pronounce anything ending with "-tor" as "-tour" instead of "ter"

- legislator becomes legislat-TOUR
- mediator becomes media-TOUR
- director becomes direc-TOUR
- realtor becomes real-TOUR

Just screw up words altogether

- naivete become naitivity
- extrapolate becomes extrasolate
- juxtaposed becomes just opposed
- Feng Shui becomes Moo Shoo

Double negatives rule

- regardless becomes irregardless
- merciless becomes unmerciless
- the unfortunate becomes the less unfortunate

Add "–ate" rule

- administer becomes administrate
- preventive become preventative
- orient becomes orientate
- converse becomes conversate

I started to make up my own words: ambitesticular, anthropomorphine, bilingitis, cankersoreity, concubenign, concubinous, convagulate, cornicopulate, deflammatory, diabotanical, flaccidassidosis, flubbergasted, inclitation, maxipedantic, obviaduct, peramblinguistic, preclucivity, pseudocervical, sorgumasticate, subcutenacious, tamborinate, tinklination, vacuumhooverous

I'd stick a made up word in a memo or email and see if anyone would notice. "Mr. Thompson challenged us to an average 60 orders in eight hours. By obviaduction, I calculate this out to be seven and a half an hour." There was one customer service clerk, Carey who graduated from

UCLA. She thought it was hilarious. After a while, I imagine most people thought I was either acting too smart for them or a complete idiot.

I then had my cat idiom phase. Whenever talking to staff, coworkers, or writing emails, I'd throw in a cat idiom like: cat's meow, cat's pajamas, catbird seat, cat on a hot tin roof, cat's whiskers, curiosity killed the cat, more than one way to skin a cat, like herding cats, sourpuss, scaredy cat, smitten as a kitten, kitten caboodle.

"Last week, we only had one order returned for an undeliverable zip code. While one is still too much, it's still the cat's pajamas compared to three returned orders in one week last month."

I had my ob- phase, throwing around words like obviate, obtuse, obstreperous, oblique, obfuscate, obsequious, obscure, obsolescence, obtrusive.

I had my coagulate and congeal phase. I'd talk about orders coagulating. I'd talk about congealing ideas. Coagulating tasks. Congealing morale.

"Don't let those orders coagulate in your box. Let me know, and I'll just pass them around. We're a team. Everyone gets those difficult orders that take forever. You can't obviate shit."

I was also making fun of all the idiots in the office throwing around all the stupid management buzzwords like: paradigm shift, proactive, put your ducks in a row, win-win, synergy, thinking outside the box, world-class, flattened hierarchy, self-directed teams, growing shit like we lived on a farm.

"I think the group dynamic starts out with one individual developing a case of synergy, because it's not an individual thing really, if one person has synergy, it can catch on quickly and infect the whole group."

I tried to introduce old school terms like: Photostat, in the final analysis, the buck stops here, far out, groovy, peachy keen, ducky, wise guys, cool beans, by the by.

"By the by, it would be ducky if we learned everyone else's job so we're not wasting our time running around trying to find out who does what, in the final analysis."

"King Lear," I said. "It's a Shakespeare play. King Lear is this dude who splits his kingdom up and shows preference to the wrong daughters and winds up being overrun by those daughters and destroying his kingdom."

"Ah," she replied. "I don't know any Shakespeare. I couldn't read it in high school."

"Well," I replied, "it's more interesting than most people think, like the story of Felatio and how he came to blows with the evil, cunning Litus in the old, city of Caligula."

They all had blank looks on their faces as I heard snickers from Carey across the office.

In hindsight, I realize I was just being an ass myself, and humoring myself at the expense of others. I graduated from Stanford and a private high school, but fact was, I was living in a weekly motel in Reno, working as a data entry supervisor. I may have been smart and well-educated, but I was in truth a complete, clueless idiot. It was the conceit of youth and self-delusion. It wasn't my fault that I was over-qualified in an entry-level job living in a weekly motel. It was society's fault. It was the economy. It was my mother. It was my bad luck. I had yet to take any responsibility for anything.

One day going over a customer's invoice, I started flirting with Carey. She seemed a bit mercurial, but then again, she was hot, so I didn't really mind. I asked her what kind of food she liked, and she was all into this Thai and Vietnamese thing. She told me the best pho in town was a place called Pho 777. I told her it should be called Pho 775, because the Reno area code was changing to 775 from 702. She didn't think that was funny. We agreed to meet up there for a date.

Pho 777 used to be down a block at a place called the Mizpah Hotel. I guess Thai and pho were all the rage in the Bay. I never jumped on that bandwagon. I enjoyed the seafood in San Francisco but mostly the Latino food: Peruvian, Mexican, El Salvadoran, Dominican, especially Papusas and Empanadas. I also liked the gigantic burritos which I often cut in half and ate for two meals. I did like the dim sum though and hanging around Chinatown. I never understood Thai and pho. Pho to me was like Ramen with basil and cilantro.

"So, you ever had pho?" She asked.

"Phu?" I imitated the way she pronounced it.

"Yes, Phu. It's not pronounced Pho."

"You know if we started to pronounce every food item in its native language, I don't think we'd ever get around to eating."

"Oh, you're such an old Euro-centric colonialist." I wasn't sure if she was serious. Often times, I wouldn't know if she was being sarcastic or serious.

"Well, seriously, it's like those reporters who are all like, 'There's a tropical storm approaching the eastern shore of Me-HE-co, and there was a shooting in Te-HU-WANA.' What if they were reporting about a story in China. They'd all be like, 'An earthquake hit the small city of Wang-Ching-Waa-Hwaa-Gong." I exaggerated the whiney sound of Mandarin or Cantonese, I'm not sure which. There's a huge Chinese population in San Francisco, and interestingly, I heard more Chinese people speaking perfect English than anywhere else in my life. It shocked me one day when I ran across a very old Chinese dude, and he sounded just like John Wayne. Seattle was more of a Japanese town, and they too had very old Japanese people who were born there and spoke perfect English.

"Stop it!" She whispered looking around.

"Don't get me started on the Vietnamese accent."

"Oh my god!"

The waiter came over, and I ordered Sweet and Sour Chicken.

"Are you kidding me?!" Her mouth dropped. "We're in a Vietnamese restaurant and you're ordering Panda Express food???" She was really loud.

"It's on the menu." I pleaded.

"Do you need more time?" the waiter asked.

"Yes," she replied, "I'm going to need to educate this boy."

"Look, I've had fuh before. I'm not too crazy about it."

"There's other Vietnamese stuff on the menu. And why did you agree to go to Pho 777 then?"

"Hey, whatever to get you out on a date."

"A date? This isn't a date."

I almost flushed with embarrassment.

"So we're splitting the check?" I asked.

"Yeah. You're not getting in my panties by buying my dinner. I don't prostitute myself for food."

"I didn't say I expected that."

"Well, all guys do."

I couldn't believe we were arguing and I hardly even knew her. I considered just getting up and leaving. I was attracted to her frankness and directness, but at this point, it was becoming annoying. I guess there's a reason you have a filter for your mouth and you use tact. I guess I was also seriously annoyed that she didn't think of this as a date. I was actually starting to blush a little with frustration.

"Look why don't you order something from the Vietnamese menu. Live life a little." She continued.

She was now sounding condescending. I didn't know whether to smile, humor her, snap back, argue, or just for spite order Sweet and Sour Chicken. You know guys put up with a lot of shit from women just to get in their panties. With her being so frank about not allowing me in her panties, my patience for her bitchy, condescending attitude was running out fast. This dinner was turning into a nightmare.

"I've had a lot of different foods in San Francisco. I don't have to eat everything on this planet to live life."

She rolled her eyes.

"Here, I'll have this," I gave in.

I had three choices: I could leave, which was becoming increasingly tempting. I could fight her and make the whole dinner unbearable, or I could just play along and make the best of it.

"Bun bo Hue. You know how to pronounce that?" I asked.

"No."

"Oh, I thought you were the expert."

"Just point to it with your finger."

"It's probably pronounced Bubba Hoo Haa."

She smiled facetiously.

"You know," I continued, "if some foreigner comes to America and orders 'hambugga' I'm not going to be offended that he doesn't call it a 'hamburger.'" I think I was beating this horse dead, but I was trying to put a humorous spin on it, offer a peace offering of sorts.

"Oh shut up." She didn't take it.

"So you know, the whole Thai thing. I noticed in San Francisco, all these Chinese restaurants, they'd just change their name to Bangkok or Thai Palace or something and throw in a few Thai dishes, you notice that?"

"So you graduated from Stanford. Why are you in Reno?"

I wasn't so sure she was being sincere or setting me up to mock me. Her whole MO was this big ornery, feisty, condescending, mocking thing. I came across quite a few of them in the Bay, just this facetious, snarky, attitude, cynical thing.

"The economy tanked. I had a friend in Reno who told me there were job opportunities here."

She laughed. "Like what? Cocktail waitress at a casino?"

"Well sure, I admit, once I got here, I realized the job opportunities had a lot to do with gaming and tourism, but still, there's a lot of California companies that come over here all the time. There's a lot of high tech stuff. Look at Full Charge."

"Full Charge is about as high tech as Footlocker."

"Well, I know, but I meant, Full Charge being a California company that moved here. So you graduated from UCLA, why are *you* here?"

"Well, after graduating from UCLA, I went to law school, USF School of Law."

"I didn't know that."

"I went there and worked at a law firm at the same time: Prick, Dickstein, and Jerkoffsky. I had a pretty heavy load. I guess I just couldn't handle the pressure. The people at the law firm were idiots, and I just never had much time to study. I had a nervous breakdown. I wound up in the hospital for a few weeks. My family lives here, so I moved out here to take a break." I was startled by her sudden confession.

"I'm sorry to hear that. Are you planning on going back to law school?"

"Yeah, my parents would love that. I'm not sure what I want to do now. I grew up watching *LA Law*. I always thought I wanted to be a lawyer, that glamorous, crazy lifestyle. It's nothing like that. There were nothing but fat, lazy bastards at the law firm, and all the young people, they weren't going out enjoying life, partying, they were all slaves. They were working 80 hour weeks. I couldn't see myself doing that, wasting my youth away so I could slow down in my late 30's and become this fat, entitled slob, taking advantage of the junior staff, trying to fuck interns. It made me sick, I mean literally I guess. I'll never forget the stench of cigars. There's got to be a better career field. So what's your story?"

I seriously thought about zinging back, "So you wound up as a Customer Service Clerk making $8/hour working 80 hour weeks with fat slobs trying to get in your pants?" She'd probably just reply, "Yeah, just like you, except you're the slob trying to get in my pants."

We placed our orders. I was still tempted to get the Sweet and Sour Chicken.

"Well, like you, I thought I knew what I was going to do, but I got disenchanted with Finance. I was never good with numbers, and I soon realized that Finance was all about numbers."

"Seriously?" Her mocking tone returned.

"I had no idea what it was about. I guess all I cared about was making a lot of money. You grew up watching *LA Law*, I grew up watching Alex P. Keaton (a teenage money-grubber on the TV show *Family Ties*) and Gordon Gekko (an adult money-grubber in the film *Wall Street*). Funny how we're influenced by pop culture. They never really showed you what they did except make deals, go to expensive lunches, party, travel in limos. You know they could make a movie about garbage men, in fact, remember, they did, with Charlie Sheen and Emilio Estevez (*Men at Work*), and they could glamorize anything, and I even bet a few kids were inspired by that movie and actually became garbage men. You know how many kids wanted to be fighter pilots after *Top Gun* came out. We're so influenced by movies. It's not like the old days, where you follow in your father's footsteps."

"My father was a Marine. I'm not about to become a fucking GI Jane (referring to the movie *GI Jane* about a woman who becomes the first female Navy SEAL which means she's a sailor not a GI Joe which is an old reference to US Army soldiers in World War II)."

"My father taught Russian literature. I could never be a professor. I'm not big into speaking in front of a large audience, and I kind of hate Russian literature. Everyone always dies in the end after a horrendously miserable life of suffering and oppression. But interestingly, I guess I sort of followed in his footsteps by wanting to become a writer."

"What do you write?"

"Well, I write fiction and nonfiction. My fiction is really weird; I guess that's the genre, just surreal stuff, bizarre -"

"What about your nonfiction?" she interrupted.

"Well, I write about human nature, society, how we're succumbing to an age of human maladaptation, where society is really disfiguring true human nature. I mean, the whole Taylorism thing, the automation, factory process is dehumanizing, the assembly line, turning humans into automatons, the emphasis on efficiency not creativity."

"You mean the whole Industrial Age."

"Well, yeah, but it's leaking into the Information Age."

"I think we're in the Biomedical Age." I had no idea what she was talking about and ignored her.

"I read a Harvard paper a while back, about centralization and decentralization, and how we've become so centralized and need to be more decentralized and autonomous."

"Platonism." I had no idea what she was talking about and ignored her again.

"I envision a new age, one where we shape society around human nature and not vice versa, where we celebrate our human qualities instead of try to suppress or medicate them out of existence."

"You mean we should embrace depression and homicidal feelings?" She was so argumentative, it was annoying.

"Well, no, you see, we have an urge to kill, and people are always saying, society teaches us not to act out on these destructive, natural feelings, but we also have a fear of being killed ourselves, or a fear of trying to kill someone and getting killed by that person. It's natural for us to want to kill, but it's also natural for us to not want to kill and to live free from the fear of being killed. I always hate it when people associate society with all our good instincts and then consider our instincts as nothing but our bad instincts."

"Like what?"

"Like love. You don't need society to teach us how to love. You see wild animals express love and compassion all the time. Mothers in the wild will sacrifice their own safety to protect their young."

"But that's selfish behavior, because she's protecting her genetic offspring."

"Well, in that sense yes, but it's also social and loving too."

"It can't be both."

"Well, there are times a mother will take in an orphan or even a baby animal of a different species."

"Doesn't mean she's selfless. She's just confused. Nature gives her the instinct to nurture babies, and 99.9% of the time, it's her own genetic offspring or a close relative. Are you a conspiracy theorist? Do you think there's this big, secret plot to oppress us? Do you believe Freemasons rule the world? Jews? Did you know that my father is both a Freemason and a Jew?"

God, she was so unbelievably obnoxious. She was now deriding me and implying I was a nut job. I was thinking I should have left while I could have, and it was still an option, but unfortunately, we worked together, and she might get all vengeful and fuck me over at work.

"Well, I certainly believe that those in power do collude, and it's just natural, who wouldn't. You can't blame them. I mean poor people collude all the time to sell stuff to each other and not pay taxes or work under the table. With rich people, it's just on a larger scale, and with the super-rich, it's on a global scale. They have power and money, and they want to keep their power and money, and there are countless people who want to take away their power and money. They have meetings, and if they're smart, they would have secret meetings. This whole thing about the Federal Reserve, I mean, it's as much a government agency as FedEx."

"You are a conspiracy theorist."

"You like labels."

"You notice how all the conspiracy theorists tend to take the bus? You take the bus don't you?"

I looked away; she knew I did.

"Are you an Atheist?"

"Oh, so now we're talking religion. Do you want to hit all the three taboo subjects for a first date and talk about sex too?"

"We're not on a date."

"Oh yeah, right."

"I'm an Atheist. God's too convenient, and if anyone takes responsibility for the suffering and misery of innocent people, that thing or entity is not good. You can have freewill without the horrors of human atrocities. In fact, make all human atrocities an illusion if all you want is to extract the good and freewill out of people. Why make it real?"

"Well, maybe it only feels real. What if all that misery was an illusion?"

"I'm pretty fucking sure it isn't, because I can feel my own misery and assuming the misery of others is an illusion makes you a narcissistic, sadistic fuck. If you think about it, we just happened to become intelligent first. It could have been insects, could have been Bonobo monkeys, then we'd all have sex instead of killing each other. So how many sexual partners have you had?"

"What is this 21 Questions?"

"It's 20 Questions. You're not a virgin are you?"

"I'm not answering all your questions. You know, as you get older, you realize you don't have to answer insincere or rhetorical questions. It's like with Howard Stern. He gets people in that trap of answering these really degrading questions, but they don't have to. I'd just ignore him."

"1 to 10? 11 to 20? 21 to 30?"

"Okay, look, you ask a woman how many guys she's been with, and you basically add ten. You ask a guy, and you divide that number by ten. So a woman will tell you, oh, five guys, and it's actually 15. A guy goes, oh about 50, and it's more like 5."

"So, how many women have you slept with?"

"70,000."

"Ha." She let up. She could have been a pretty damn good trial lawyer, the bitch. "I've been with 70 guys."

"Serious?"

"When I was in college and law school, I supplemented my income by working as an escort."

Right at that moment, the waiter brought us our food. She was unapologetic.

"It was good money. I mean come on, with the price of textbooks these days? I was also a dominatrix, and you'd be surprised how many powerful executives, politicians, and lawyers want some woman to bitch slap them and yank them around with a dog leash. Willie Brown (then mayor of San Francisco) he liked to cry a lot and dress up in diapers. Great tipper."

"Can I get you anything else?" the waiter asked.

"I think we're fine," I replied.

"I'm just kidding." She dug into her pho. I wasn't sure what to believe.

Chapter 4: Lust

Needless to say, I never went out with Carey again. One late night, Marla came over. She had been staying late. She was on salary. All the salary folks and managers were making a good effort of coming in late but before Mr. Thompson and then staying as late as him until 8 PM often. But after 5 PM, after the hourly staff went home, all they did was socialize and kiss up to Sam. This was their recreation. The hourlies would go home and watch TV, exercise, have hobbies, go to bars, gamble. The managers would just all shoot the breeze, hide in their offices goofing off, perhaps napping, or follow Sam around as he ranted about something or another. I never got a work-related email from any of them after 5 PM.

Marla and Sam had a bizarre relationship. Sometimes they would fight in jest and sometimes it would be for real. Most of the times, if you pissed off Sam, you got fired. Marla got a pass. She could be rather frank and direct with Sam, but not always. Sometimes I'd ask her to tell Sam something frankly and honestly, and she could. She became my conduit with Sam. I was finishing up some data entry by myself and sample checking my staff's work when she came by and sat on my desk with her legs a few inches from me.

"Hey there Mr. Bill."

She liked calling me that. It was flirtatious. For whatever reason, people regress to baby-speech when they become intimate. It has some weird psychological effect on you, making you feel vulnerable, cared for, nurtured. Sometimes, however, when you were not the target of the baby talk, it would be unbearably irritating. I don't know if that was jealousy however as opposed to simple annoyance. The managers also became significantly more informal after 5 PM acting like juvenile screwballs.

"Hey Marla. How's it going?" I finished off an order.

"You've been working a lot lately."

I was getting rich off overtime. I had even bought a used car.

"Oh yeah. Well, you know, I can process fifteen orders an hour. It doesn't make sense to me to have someone else processing five orders an hour. Even with overtime pay, it's more cost-effective-"

"Yeah, but you need a social life too."

I looked up at her. She was playing with one of my fast food toys. I used to have a good diet in high school, but I just let myself go in college and after. Working long hours didn't help. I didn't have time to make food at home or relax at a restaurant. I just drove down the street to grab fast food and inhaled it. I was also starting to drink espresso. Data entry is quite possibly the most boring job in the world next to being a security guard at a warehouse, but high on caffeine, time flew by. It was actually a perfect job for me. It was mindless, and I could use my mind for other purposes and goals in life.

"But I'll get one more temp, and I think we won't need as much overtime." I looked deeply into her eyes. "I don't have much of a social life at the moment anyway."

She smiled and looked away. I started to wonder if she noticed that I now had an erection with her sitting so close to me. I hadn't had sex in a year – or two. I knew she was married, but my mind was on high speed. It was barreling through on caffeine and all the chaos and change, and morality, responsibility, they just seemed to be so abstract and immaterial and oblique. All I could think about was processing orders, supervising, excellence, high speed, Marla, sex, Andrea in customer service. It was like I was regressing to some primitive, primate state. I stopped writing my philosophy book. I didn't do anything when I went home. I just ate, watched TV and crashed. I had no friends in Reno. Like a lot of the managers, my social life was work. If I wanted a friend or a date, it would have to come from work.

"Well, maybe we can just hang out some time," she offered.

"Yeah, that sounds fun. You know, I really didn't get to know you much in San Francisco. I had a lot of fun there."

"Oh yeah, it was crazy. You know, I remember the first day you came in."

"Oh yeah."

"I was thinking to myself. That guy will only last –," her eyes rolled up, "oh three days at most. We had a pool going."

"Really?"

"No," she laughed. "I'm just messing with you." She touched my arm.

I loved the way Marla laughed. She was in her 30's and married, so I never even fantasized about making out with her, but then I noticed the way she would flirt with Mr. Thompson and some of the other managers, and I was thinking to myself, maybe she would cheat on her husband. All the sudden, she moved from one category to the other, from "unattainable waste of time" to "possibility." I started to look at her differently. I started to notice her beauty. I started to notice her charming little expressions and gestures. They were almost girlie. She was like a 14 year-old in a 30-something body, all awkward, childish, and playful. One time, she had her back to the wall and arms spread across the wall, and the sun was setting on her, and she looked like a supermodel or a goddess. I don't know if she knew I was staring at her, but I wanted to burn that image into my mind for all eternity. It's still glowing there.

"Well, I thought you'd make it a long time," I came back, "years, maybe decades. Maybe you'd retire from the company in your 70's or something. They'd give you a crystal bowl or something, and you'd slip your disc carrying it home, drop it, slip on the broken glass and break your hip, get a hernia trying to get up. It would be ironic."

She laughed loudly. You could often hear her across the length of the entire office all the way to the back office next to the warehouse. Sometimes I wondered if she did it on purpose to get attention. Sometimes a hot Marketing clerk or secretary would come along, and she had this affected way of being really nice to her, but you would know deep down, she wanted to get rid of her as soon as possible, and often, she would. She was the queen bee at this place. Everyone knew it. The last thing she needed was Mr. Thompson distracted by a hot, young babe.

"You're so funny, you should be a comedian."

"You know actually, I thought about being a stand-up comic."

I'm not sure she thought I was being serious or not, but I actually had. I was a good comic writer, but I'm not sure I would have enjoyed the performance part and trying to remember all my jokes.

"What do you want to be when you grow up?" I asked.

She smiled. I'm not sure if she got the jab.

"I've always been fascinated by Marketing. You can have the best product in the world, but if you don't know how to communicate its value, no one will use it."

"Oh yeah. The greatest inventors often died penniless. And the greatest scientific discoveries are often attributed to the wrong person. It's not what you know but who you know or how you sell it."

"I wasn't always in Marketing. I had a mentor who hired me for a few years and taught me Marketing. Before that, I worked in the casinos. I did accounting and cashiering. I dealt blackjack for a bit."

"Really? We'll have to go down to the casinos, and you can teach me how to beat the house."

"Oh, there's no beating the house my friend." She touched the back of my hand. "You can play the perfect blackjack game and over time, you'll lose and you'll always be behind. I didn't like taking people's money like that. It was sad. Some of the guys would just keep losing and losing, and I'd feel so bad for them. Sure it was fun when they win, but most of the time I was just taking their money. I got a lot of players, you know, they thought I was cute. But I had a feeling not all of them could afford it. I'd see guys walk off and come back with a whole bunch of twenties. They were taking money out on credit. Many don't even play the perfect game. It was just all too sad."

"Well, I'm glad you got out of it. Doesn't sound like a fun job."

"What about you? What did you do before here?"

"Um, don't you remember? You interviewed me."

She laughed. She cocked her head to one side.

"Do you have any idea how many people we interviewed? Oh my gosh! Okay, I remember you graduated from Stanford, and you like to write."

"I was also King of England for a few months, but I always felt like I was working in a fish bowl. I quit without giving them a two week notice. For a few weeks, England had no king or queen, and you know what, the world didn't end."

She laughed.

"Yeah, and I also went to jail for a couple years for drug trafficking," I continued. "I worked at Burger King for a few weeks. I didn't put this all on my resume of course."

"Oh, I can't imagine why."

"Yeah, but I turned stateside, and testified against this big Mexican drug cartel boss, and they reduced my sentence and changed my name and sent me to Reno. I mean come on; why else would anyone live in Reno?"

"Oh my God."

"Yeah, that's my life's story. I was an orphan, spent my time in an orphanage, sang a lot, found out my dad was a billionaire, and then I went to Stanford but then just screwed up my life." It was partially true.

"I spent some time in foster homes."

"Really?" I always wonder about how inappropriate that response is. I can imagine someone going, "Oh no, not really, I was just kidding about that tragedy." Or if they just said, "I just found out my mother died in a car accident." I would respond, "Really?" And they'd be all like, "No, just kidding. Haha. She was actually murdered. Some dude broke into her house, raped her, and then slit her throat and she bled out. But that car thing, that was just a joke. Did you like it? Was it funny?"

"My mother was crazy. She was really religious, and she'd always accuse me of being a moral degenerate. I could never bring my friends over. She was really abusive and an alcoholic. She had wild rages where she'd tear up my clothes calling me a whore and a sinner. For a few years I just went from one foster home to another."

"That's awful." I was surprised by her candor. I was getting a little tired too. Fatigue was setting in. Perhaps with her too, fatigue was blowing away her discretion.

"But you know what; my friends helped me get through it all. I stayed with them until I could get my own place and worked in a casino. But you know, I think it was all meant to be. I sympathize more with people who are sick mentally. I understand their situation. But it's all in the past. You can't change the past. You can't get stuck in the past."

"Yeah, I read somewhere, you can't control the past or future, just a few seconds in the future, the time it takes you to turn an observation into a perception into a judgment into an action. I also read a study somewhere that you could get addicted to grief." I instantly felt stupid for saying this, acting all detached nerdy instead of compassionate. Later in the day, I noticed I was becoming increasingly impulsive and tended to say whatever I was thinking. I even got in an argument with some guy over the stupidest thing, perceiving that the way he answered my question was disrespectful. Working late was changing me.

"I met a pit boss at the casino."

"Pit boss?"

"Yeah, they work the tables. They watch the floormen who in turn watch the dealers. Everyone is watching everyone else. The eye in the sky, they watch everyone: employees, dealers, gamblers, everyone."

"Wow, it's kind of creepy."

"Oh yeah, whenever you walk into a casino, there's someone checking you out. Checking out how you walk, what you're wearing, where you walk, what you're looking at, whether you go to the bar or a slot or a table. They're watching you!" She emphasized with her eyes.

"So, I married the guy, but I left the casino and went into Marketing. Things didn't go so well after that. I knew he liked to gamble when I married him, but I had no idea he was such an addict. It was pretty bad. We never could get anything of value. It would be gone within weeks. He'd get a new car, gone in a few months. New motorcycle, gone. New boat, gone. New laptop, gone. He even pawned his wedding ring once. I made sure to keep our bank accounts separate. He was also really possessive and always wanted to know who I was with, where I was, where I was going. He always thought I was cheating on him. It was really the other way around. I'm pretty sure he was seeing a couple women at the casino. But he always turned it around and accused me. He gets really verbally abusive and one time he got physical. He had to take this domestic violence class, and he blamed me for it. He accused me of being the abuser and showed me how I did all these things to manipulate and insult him."

"That's what abusers do. I read a book about that in college. They turn themselves into the victims. They make you feel guilty. Why don't you just divorce the guy?"

She rolled her eyes.

"It's just complicated. We have a kid together. He's threatened to take her from me. Sometimes I think he's really trying to make an effort. I don't know. I still love him. There are times he can be so funny, so good, so kind. Sometimes I think I can just go to work and get away and not deal with it. Sometimes I think I'm the problem. If I'm not there, there's no problem."

"Well, the German people loved Hitler at first, and at first he was quite charming. Look how that turned out?"

She smiled.

"Is that why you always work so late?" I asked. "To get away from him?"

"Well that and Mr. Thompson. He's trying to get me involved in all aspects of the company not just Marketing. He really wants to integrate me into the company and capture the Marketing aspect in everything that

43

we do. He's trying to take the company public. It's not a secret. I can tell you. We all have the opportunity here to make a LOT of money."

"Huh, wow."

"There's a lot of changes he's planning. He'll inform everyone later. It's a little crazy though. It's like he wants me to wear two hats, and I only get paid for one."

"That sucks."

She looked at her watch. "It's getting late."

"Yeah." I looked at my computer screen. I wanted to talk with her all night long until the Customer Service Reps showed up first in the morning to get the east coast calls.

"It was nice talking to you Bill." She put a hand on my shoulder. I was tempted to put a hand on her knee, perhaps up her skirt. I was fatigued and impulsive, but I wasn't stupid. I let it be.

"Yeah, I really enjoyed talking with you. Anytime you want to hang out, let me know."

"Definitely." Her tone was serious and more mature now.

She gave me a little, one-handed shoulder massage.

"Get some rest will ya. I'll see you tomorrow," she left. I had an erection again.

I couldn't sleep that night. I had fallen for her. My heart bled for her. I just imagined her with her crazy mother and now her crazy husband. I also had a crazy mother, and I felt that was why we seemed to bond so deeply.

After a few weeks of flirting late night in the office, she agreed to come over to my place, and I offered her a drink. She grabbed a beer. She sat on my couch. My mind was racing. I couldn't quiet it down. I was wondering if I should make the moves or wait for her. I fantasized about her going into my bedroom and taking off her clothes. Would it just be spontaneous? Would I have to make the first move? Would I have to cross the line first toward infidelity? What was infidelity? Would I feel guilty? Would I get bad karma? Would I get married and would my wife cheat on me?

It was awkward at first; we talked about work. She then suggested we grab a bite, and I was surprised when she suggested pizza. It didn't seem very romantic. We went to Blind Onion. The waiter was totally screwy, and he screwed up our order, but I was thinking, I'd probably score more points by laughing it off than getting really annoyed and talking to the manager. We wound up eating this weird white cheese, garlic pizza. I basically interviewed her the whole time, and since then, I realized that it doesn't turn women on when you interrogate them the whole date. They want to get to know you. A woman's defenses come down when they feel comfortable and familiar around you, and the only way that happens is when you disclose yourself to them, and make them pity you or sympathize with you, not the other way around.

She told me a lot of personal secrets. She suffers from both depression and insomnia. She said the pain of her depression feels like a thousand pin pricks on her back. Time just flew, and I started to notice that we were the only two left there. It was one of those classic romantic moments. I drove her back to my place, and walked her to her car. I thought I was just blowing it. Why didn't she want to come inside? I offered her another drink. She said she needed to get back home.

She gave me a hug, and I grabbed her head and kissed her.

She didn't resist. The worst case scenario, she would have pulled back and screamed. "What the fuck? Bill?! What the fuck?! Are you kidding me?! I'm married! Oh my God! I'm married Bill! I'm not going to commit adultery with you, you crazy fuck!! Oh my God! I'm married Bill! This is sexual harassment Bill! We work together remember!"

I just mouth fucked her with my tongue.

I slid my hand down her shirt. I slid my hand under her bra and began rubbing her nipple. She pulled back a little.

"Bill, I can't."

I kissed her hard again, and just rubbed her breast. I put my thigh hard up into her crotch and grinded. She moaned. I unbuttoned her jeans. I hate jeans. It's pretty obvious if a woman wears jeans on a first date, it's like armor. They're the hardest things to get off a woman I swear to god. You need three hands and a crowbar not to mention figuring out how to get their shoes off first.

I went right down and rubbed her wet. I don't know about you, but if you don't know whether the outfielder is going to chase your ball down, why not run the bases as fast as you can.

"Oh Bill, God no." She pushed me back. I unbuttoned my jeans and surprised myself when I took out my penis. Was I going to fuck her right there against her car without a condom? She buttoned up her jeans.

"Bill."

I grabbed her and kissed her again and just grinded up against her jeans. I'd regret that later when I found some blood stains in my underwear from a small gash on my penis. You'd think your penis would have thicker skin, but then again, I guess you wouldn't feel anything then. I suppose that's why you're not supposed to try to fuck a woman through her jeans. After a car drove by, I realized that I could get in trouble exposing myself in public.

"Hey, I could get arrested for this. Why don't we go to my place?"

"No, no, I can't."

"Okay, how about at least in the back of your car?"

She paused. It seemed like forever. She turned around and opened the back car door. I had heard about people fucking in the backseat of their cars, but I never had and always wondered what it might be like. As it turns out, the backseat of a car is not designed for one person lying down, much less two.

She lay down on her back and spread her legs wide. I jumped on top of her. We made out, and I started getting hot so I took off my jacket and then I tried to take her jeans off, but she resisted.

"No, no, no!" I had a flashback to sex ed class when they say "no" means "no." The last thing I'd ever do was rape a woman. She didn't need to be so firm about it. It wasn't like I was, well I guess, I was being a bit aggressive. It never really occurred to me until a woman told me that women have it hard. Not only do they have to defend themselves against other women always trying to put them down and spread rumors about them, but they have to physically defend themselves constantly against guys trying to get in their pants. It's like a pretty boy being in prison, always fighting off dudes trying to rape him.

"Okay, fine, fine." I assured her. I started rubbing my own penis. She then grabbed it and started jerking me off.

I started humping her as if I had put it in. She started moaning wildly. I grabbed her breast with one hand and the back of her head with the other. I was thinking about coming, but I just couldn't all crammed up in here, and my dick wasn't even in her. I don't know where my dick was at this point. We were just dry humping. I was getting hot and tired. I unbuttoned my shirt. I couldn't seem to get the last buttons off, or I was just too lazy. I started dry humping her again. But I was too tired, and I was a little annoyed at not being able to penetrate her. I pulled myself up. I took a few deep breaths. I looked at the car and noticed the windows fogged up.

"I'm sorry," she said.

"No, you don't have to be sorry."

"I'm sorry. I'm so sorry. I'm really sorry."

"No, you just need to get divorced. I honestly think you should leave the guy. Just get divorced and we'll get together. Just divorce the guy."

"I'm sorry. I'm sorry."

"You don't have to be sorry."

"I'm sorry for saying I'm sorry."

I started to button my shirt up and look for my jacket.

She got up too. I started kissing her again.

"Oh god I want to so badly," she said.

"Okay, I gotta go." I hugged her and got out the back of the car.

"I had a good time," I said awkwardly. "Drive safely."

"I will."

I wobbled back to my place, buzzing with a little headache. There was pressure in my sinuses. I felt weird and odd and strange. I grabbed a beer and sat on my couch dazed. I didn't even turn on the TV or lights. I was just dazed. I didn't cross the line, but I had crossed some line. I mean, what would have stopped me from having sex with her except she stopped me.

Chapter 5: Tweaker

I started to obsess about Marla, but she moved on to her next flavor of the month, a guy she hired to be her secretary. He was married too. Marla just loved men's attention. She teased him just like she teased me. Maybe her mother was right about her. She stopped coming by my cubicle. Sometimes I'd work late on purpose, just to get the chance to run into her, but she never talked to me like she did before. I became angry and resentful toward her and thought up ways of undermining her and making Sam realize she was nothing but a slutty idiot using him. I even considered calling her husband and anonymously telling him that she was sleeping with Sam. It was driving me mad with rage and jealousy, but one night when the customer service staff was all hanging out celebrating one of their birthdays, I wound up talking to Andrea, a hot customer service clerk. She invited me out to their party after work at Trader Dick's at the Nugget in Sparks. We danced on the dance floor, and she held me so tight. It was the most amazing thing. I stopped thinking about Marla altogether. Andrea was hotter and younger than Marla. Dating Andrea would definitely make Marla jealous. Time stood still. We were in each other's embrace. I don't know how many songs went by. We were actually spinning a little bit, and I was honestly getting a little dizzy, but I didn't mind. I had fallen in love with Andrea. She was holding me as if we were on the edge of a cliff, and she was deathly afraid of falling over the edge.

We went out to dinner the next week. I took her to Beaujolais, a fancy French restaurant downtown. I don't think she had ever been to such a nice place. I had rabbit. She ordered chicken. She had escargot for the first time in her life. I had to almost force one down her throat. She almost gagged. I assured her she would get used to it with time.

"You know the thing I noticed about Reno people," I told her. "Well, people in general. If you don't live near the coast, you generally don't like seafood, and it makes sense. Like back in the day before refrigeration, if you grew up inland, and you come across shellfish, well, you probably shouldn't eat it."

"I don't mean to be so white trash."

"Oh no, no. You're not. It's just something in general. I mean, I grew up near Seattle, and seafood was everywhere. You just have to get an early taste for it. What surprises me, however, is how many all-you-can-eat sushi places Reno has."

"Yeah, it's kind of weird right."

"I mean, I guess it has to do with competing against all the all-you-can-eat casino buffets, but seriously, how can you possibly trust seafood that is all-you-can-eat?"

"I've never had sushi. I tried it once, and it was just squishy and gross."

"You know, I always wonder why they don't have like beef, pork, or chicken sushi. I mean, wouldn't that be great? Slices of rib-eye rolled up with a cucumber, lettuce, rice, and wrapped in seaweed?"

"Hmmm. I guess if sushi was like that, I'd try it."

"Well, they have fried sushi, would you try that?"

"Yeah, sure, that's like cooked fish right?" I was thinking to myself that it was obvious that fried fish is cooked fish, but I wasn't about to be an idiot and tell her that.

"So you were born and raised here?"

"I was born in Winnemucca."

"Where's that?"

"It's about 160 miles east on 80 (Interstate 80). It's a really small town. But we moved to Reno when I was seven, so I don't really remember much about Winnemucca."

"You plan on staying in Reno?"

"Oh hell no, my god. The first chance I get, I'm out of here. You know how much I would have loved to go to San Francisco." Andrea was hired after the company moved to Reno. "One day maybe or New York City."

"What would you do in New York City?"

"Singing. I love to sing. I made a demo tape in high school. I've sung at a few hockey games (back when Reno had a minor league hockey team). It's just something I love doing. I know it's a pretty hard business to get into, but you know, if you just try, go and try to make your dreams come true, I think that's the important thing. I mean I could be a waitress or customer service clerk in Reno and not pursue my dreams, or I could be a waitress or customer service clerk in New York City and pursue my dreams."

"I think you're absolutely right. I mean, I want to be a published author someday, but in my case, I can do that in any city. But I guess, when I get the chance, when the economy turns around, I'll hit San Francisco again."

"I think you should try your best to get published. What do you write?"

"Oh, it's esoteric strange shit."

"I'd love to read it sometime."

"Sure." Truth was everything was on the drawing board. I had short stories I had written in college, but I hadn't written anything since then in fiction. I had started to write a nonfiction book on society and human nature, I guess, a conspiracy theory according to Carey. It was book length, but I hadn't tried to get it published yet. Maybe Carey was right. Maybe I was a crazed lunatic riling against the evils of society.

"I'd love to hear you sing some time."

She smiled.

We then went dancing at Reno Live, and I kissed her when we sat down. It was just amazing. I imagined her being my girlfriend. I imagined making Marla jealous of us as we flirted with each other at work. I sent her flowers the following week, delivered to her desk. I didn't want everyone in the office knowing we were dating, so I just signed the card, "Thank you for dinner and dancing." The flowers definitely caught Marla's attention, and Marla asked her who the lucky guy was. I don't think Andrea told her, but it would have been cool if she had.

That Friday, however, Andrea canceled our date, and she didn't call to make it up on Saturday. I spent the whole weekend upset with an aching feeling in my gut literally. I couldn't concentrate. I felt depressed, angry. I shitted out everything I ate. I didn't know what to do. Should I keep calling her? Should I fight for her? Was she testing me? Was she trying to play hard to get? Should I give her some space? I just didn't know what to do. I asked some coworkers without telling them it was Andrea. They all gave me the expected advice. *Have faith. She may just need time. It will all work out.* There was only one coworker, Carey, who was frank and honest, but a bit too frank and honest. She told me to figure it out, "she's just not that into you. Get over it." Carey could be a bitch sometimes, but she was also dead on right. Sometimes I considered dating Carey, but she was too crazy for me with her mood swings. She just scared the fuck out of me.

I wasn't sure what to do on Monday. I didn't want to confront Andrea at work. I didn't want anyone there to know we were dating. I didn't want to embarrass her. I also felt annoyed, and I thought if I just ignored her, she might wonder if I was still interested in her. At the end of every day, I held out hope that she might come by just to say hi and chitchat, say something to me, anything. At the end of every day, I'd walk over to customer service, and they would all be gone. She was purposefully avoiding me. I wondered what I had done. Did I say something? Did I do something? Why did she come on to me so fast and then just as quickly let it all disappear and evaporate? I hated the uncertainty. At times, I just wanted to clear things up, confront her. Is it over? Do you need a break? I just didn't want to face the reality that she might actually say, yes, it's over, I'm sorry, I'm seeing someone else, I changed my mind, I'm over you. I oscillated between the hell of reality and the fantasy of her coming around, grabbing me, telling me she actually loved me after all.

That weekend, I called her, and she never returned my messages. Friday night passed. Saturday night passed. A bunch of coworkers and I had set up the following weekend to go to San Francisco, and I agreed thinking that it would be a great opportunity to take Andrea and show her around. That weekend, I was supposed to take Andrea, share a hotel room with her, make love to her all night and in the morning. I had it all planned out, but the week just passed by, and before I knew it, I was flying out to San Francisco without her. I was devastated. The whole weekend, I couldn't stop thinking about her. Nothing was fun except a few moments of alcohol buzz. Otherwise, everything just seemed so boring and stupid. I even looked at my coworkers who were having fun and telling me stories, and I just wanted to tell them all to shut the fuck up. I hated life. Everything was meaningless and bland. I hated my job. I hated my vacation. San Francisco usually got me all excited, but this weekend, it seemed emptier, more cold, dark, and ugly. Then finally, on Sunday, our last day there, she returned my call. She agreed to go out when I got back. I was the happiest guy in the world. My stomach ache went away. It was like the clouds parted and the sun came out. I was so happy, so relieved. It was like I just gave birth to a 10 pound shit. Funny how my mood just swung around 180 degrees.

I bought her a scarf in San Francisco and met up with her at Wingfield Park. We walked around a while and then sat on the grass. She then told me how she had been sexually abused as a teenager, and she was afraid of getting in a relationship with me. I told her, that we could take our time, and I just enjoyed being with her, and I didn't have any expectations, but I did want to see her more. We went out again Friday night and kissed. We went out to sing karaoke, and since she was an aspiring singer, I expected her to really belt out some songs, but she was timid and barely on key. It just occurred to me then how deluded she was. Moving to New York to become a singer? She was living in a fantasy world. I sort of felt sorry for her. I told her she sang great, probably like everyone else in her life.

The following week, she didn't return any of my calls. Another week passed. Another week passed. Then Jamie, a customer service clerk who had also gone to San Francisco, approached me and asked to talk to me outside. Jamie and I had hung out a few times in San Francisco and then back in Reno. I wasn't attracted to her, but she was fun to be around. She told me that she was friends with Andrea's brother, and she was just purely looking out for me. She told me that she knew I was seeing

Andrea and didn't know if we were still going out, but that she knew for a fact that Andrea was using meth. She just told me to be careful, to wear protection. I told her that we weren't seeing each other anymore.

The next week, Andrea had quit, and Jamie approached me again. She told me that Andrea was having problems with her roommates, and they were harassing her and wouldn't leave the apartment. They weren't paying rent, and Andrea was just having a hard time dealing with the whole situation. She told me one of the roommates was a drug dealer. Jamie told me that she wanted to go down there with Andrea's brother and help her out. I agreed to help out, and I probably should not have, but I was obsessed with Andrea. I figured that she stopped seeing me because of all these roommate problems. I didn't even seem to care that she was doing meth or the possibility that her roommates weren't really the problem.

Preparing for the raid was a little adventure. I grabbed my Glock that I had just bought, filled a bag with pepper spray, a crowbar, and some handcuffs. I was ready for war. It's kind of funny how working long hours kind of fucks with your judgment. I was ready to go fucking kill someone. I was preparing for a big confrontation with a drug dealer who was probably armed, and fantasized about shooting his ass, just like that freak in *Taxi Driver*. We met up and then all drove to her apartment. I had never even been to her apartment. Her brother went up, and she let him in, and then Jamie and I went up. There was no big hug for me, no smile, no great welcome. Jamie and her brother talked to her more. I was watching the door and windows. When Andrea said that they still had keys to the apartment, I told her she should just change the locks. It seemed like a no brainer to me. I then offered to go down to the hardware store myself and go buy and install new door locks. I sped down there, came back, and installed the new door locks. On the way back, I considered taking one of the keys. There were a set of four. She wouldn't know if there were three or four. I decided not to. Why the fuck would I ever be entering her apartment without her permission? Was I nuts?

Later that evening, one of her roommates returned, and he couldn't get in. I thought it was funny. I swung the door open to his surprise and asked him what he wanted. He was a pretty muscular guy surprisingly, but I was amped up. I had Andrea's brother behind me. I was also angry that Andrea had dumped me, and may even be fucking this guy. I told him that Andrea was kicking him out, and he needed to get all his stuff out now. Surprisingly, he didn't argue with anything. Surprisingly, he started taking all his stuff outside. Her other roommate then showed up. She was the other roommate's girlfriend. Jamie then called the police to make sure there would be no problems. I figured if this dude was a dealer, the cops might ID him and bust him on an outstanding warrant or something, maybe search him and find a gun.

In my twisted, desperate mind, I was Andrea's savior. I helped Andrea fix her problem, and she would take me back. Andrea's brother set up an intervention later that week, and in hindsight, I had no business being there, but I went along. I confronted Andrea, being the bad guy, telling her that being treated like shit was no reason to treat others like shit and turn her back on her family. I was actually talking more about turning her back on me. Supposedly, Andrea cleaned up. She came back to work a week later, and she seemed to look better and happier. We never went out again. Even when I went and hung out with Jamie in the lunch room and Andrea was there, Andrea completely ignored me. What the fuck, had I meant nothing to her?

There was an interesting thing her roommate's girlfriend told me as I helped them take all their stuff outside. She told me that Andrea wasn't exactly an angel, and Andrea had told them it was okay to leave their stuff there. They weren't even living there. Andrea just made all that bullshit up as an excuse to do meth and miss work. Andrea was just as much of a user as any meth head out there. Andrea had used me. Addicts just do whatever it takes to please you, say whatever you want to hear, tell you the whole victim story, make you feel sorry for them, make you fall in love with them. Every hero needs a victim, and every victim needs a hero, but it's just a stupid codependent dance. I couldn't save Andrea, and she didn't want to be saved. We just used each other to temporarily fill our own emptiness, our voids. I wanted to use Andrea to get back at Marla. Perhaps I wasn't the angel either.

Chapter 6: Envy, Pride, and Wrath

There was a huge buzz around the office when Mr. Thompson announced that Full Charge was going public. There had been a number of suits walking around the company for quite some time. Mr. Thompson always told us that they were bankers and investors. Mr. Thompson also announced an employee stock option program, and rumor was we could quadruple our money. Everyone was seeing dollar signs. Some workers considered taking out second mortgages. My mother had died recently, and I got $15K. Why couldn't she have died before I wound up in a weekly motel? I had put it in a mutual fund, but I cashed it all out and bought 3,000 shares at $5.00 a share.

They changed the named from Full Charge to eGo. I guess that was the trend of the day. Everything was e- something. Mr. Thompson also had a huge ego, so maybe he purposefully wanted to create a rather stupid, audacious name. Mr. Thompson had kept most of this secret. I knew some of this through Marla. The company would be transformed into a mostly website driven company.

Investing in eGo was almost like gambling. My heart was beating fast as I signed the papers. We all had a big party when the company went public. In a few days, the stock was trading at around $8. My $15K investment just turned into $24K. I only wished I had invested more. Things moved pretty quickly from there. There would be a new management team from New York and Chicago, but Mr. Thompson would remain the President and retained 15% of the shares in the company.

We had an orientation with the new management team. These guys were the big boys. They had nice, new rental cars and the older ones had nice, expensive suits. Their ages ranged from 20's to 40's. The younger ones wore polo shirts. Sean Claude Lefort stuck out as the alpha of the pack. He was slick. He was from Chicago and graduated from the Booth School at the University of Chicago. He worked for Boston Consulting Group and then had head hunters offering him management positions at companies that just went public. His last job was working for an online, airline reservation website. He had the most charismatic speech of them all.

"This is a new age. This is a game changer folks. The Internet is changing the world, and most commercial transactions will occur on the Internet in the future. Internet companies are popping up like crazy, but the talent is spread thin. You may think that you can close your eyes and throw a dart at a stock listing and hit a winner, but you're dead wrong. Do you know that the first railroad and airline companies never made a profit? Who made the profits? Those who came later and consolidated the railroads and airlines and provided peripheral services to those industries: the metal producers, the steam engine makers, the airplane seat manufacturers. We don't want to be pioneers. We want to be the consolidators and industry leaders. Our goal is to grow fast quickly, grab a huge chunk of the market, and either sell to a larger company or buy out smaller companies and become the largest company in the market. But speed is the key here. We need to sprint out of the gates. The difference between us and the competition is twofold. First, the existing battery supply businesses, they may be bigger than us, but they're not on the Internet. They're resisting change. They're going to be dinosaurs like IBM and Apple. Second, the new companies, they have no idea what batteries are, and even worse, they have no idea how to run, organize, and develop a business. We have a huge advantage over the competition. We just hired five website developers and programmers. We will dominate the Internet battery selling business. We have the capital. We have one of the best management teams money can buy. This is the A team folks. It doesn't get any better than this. Not only the best and brightest, but the most aggressive and ambitious.

Now, you may look at me in my polo shirt and khaki's and wonder, how the hell do I know what I'm doing. Well, in today's market, my friend, you throw out the old textbooks. It's a whole new world folks. It's all about innovation, creativity, and speed. No offense to my older colleagues here, but you will not recognize the work world of the future. It's not about crunching numbers and productivity. It's about networks, business deals, connectivity, information, ideas. It's about business lunches, casual, fun, youthful energy. We're going to have fun. We're going to play basketball for lunch, have yoga classes, childcare. You're not going to think going to work is about going to work. It's not work anymore. It's creation. You go to a place, where every minute of every day, you are creating something new, new processes, new methods, new networks, new relationships, new designs, new ideas, new systems, new clients, new customers. You don't work hard, you don't work smart, you don't even work. You create. You become a creator, everyone, from executives and managers all the way down to the janitors. You create."

I was thinking to myself, what does a janitor really create? A clean office?

A lot of people adapted well to the new team. They were rather friendly and charismatic. I started to realize that the key to success was not just intelligence and hard work but charisma and social aptitude, the ability to make others comfortable and trust you. That's what these guys had. That's why these guys got to where they were, making over a hundred thousand a year with stock options. I was surrounded by poor people. I watched Jerry Springer. The difference between the poor and rich was not just intelligence, luck, hard work, studying, sacrifice. The big difference was social aptitude. Rich people had social graces and charm. They made deals. Business transactions were about deals. You need people you can get along with and trust. They were smooth. It was easy talking to them, chatting with them. Within a few minutes, you wanted to tell them your life's story. They just brought out that warm and fuzzy in you. They acted like they knew you your whole life.

Unfortunately, no matter how charming the executives were, the warehouse guys resisted the most. No coincidence, they were not the most educated, and had an instinctive distrust of the highly educated management team. Of course, their distrust was justified. I knew the plans to get rid of most of them and replace them with people who knew how to work with computers for the new computerized just-in-time, inventory system and then Mexican immigrants for the hard work.

The management team wasn't exactly charming with them either. They didn't like the old, gruff, fat dudes lollygagging about, taking long breaks, smoking in back, throwing foul language and sex talk around. They were the antithesis of the management team. It was a huge cultural gap. It was even odder that one of the managers was black with an MBA and most of the warehouse guys in Reno were white with GED's if they were lucky. There was also a visceral, primal conflict when the warehouse got a young, hot temp, and she preferred the management guys to the warehouse guys. For the first time, it was becoming clear to them: they were at the bottom of the food chain. It had been a pretty egalitarian place before, and Reno was a pretty egalitarian city, but with these Chicago and New York professionals, it was pretty clear who was at the very top, and who was at the very bottom. There were a couple Mexican guys who had no problem. As far as they were concerned, they didn't care about being at the bottom in America, because making American income, they allowed their families back home to rise from the bottom of Mexico. But the white dudes in Reno, sheltered from the big city, were face-to-face with the reality now. They were bottom feeders.

Gary was the most vocal of the warehouse crew. He openly insulted the management staff whenever they came through. He got along with me and saw me as a fellow blue collar even though now I was part of middle management. I identified with him more even though I went to college. He was loud, boisterous and fun and loved to make sexual jokes and often took his guys to strip clubs for lunch. He was a casting company's dream biker dude with a long, white beard, beer belly, tats, riding a Harley. The first time I met him, I thought we wouldn't get along, but you really should never judge a person by their appearances. He couldn't have been a nicer, friendlier, fun-loving, carefree dude.

One day, however, Ann, a senior accounting manager, was checking on inventory and one of the warehouse dudes, Tom said something inappropriate. Sean was livid. He went out immediately and demanded to see Tom and have him fired. Gary stepped in and told him Ann was a lying bitch, and if he knew what was good for him, he should let it go and leave.

Word spread pretty quickly and soon, a dozen other people and I were in the warehouse seeing what was going on. All the warehouse guys were standing behind Gary as he squared off with Sean. Gary was probably a good 300 lbs and 6 foot and change. He was in his late 40's or early 50's who knew the way he smoked. He probably wasn't in good shape, but he had huge biceps from lifting shit in warehouses and wrenching all his life. Sean was a lean, muscular 200 lbs and change maybe and 6 foot 2. He was 29 years old. I'm not sure how much he worked out, but he didn't seem to have any fat on his body. It was an interesting matchup. I could easily see Gary just sit on the guy and beat his brains out. I'm not sure how things would pan out if that happened. Would the warehouse guys pull him off? Would the managers jump in and start a brawl? What the fuck would I do then? Where was my loyalty? Would I try to break them apart as a peacemaker? I could wait a few minutes until the managers got their asses handed to them and then step in. Would someone call the police?

Sean smiled at Gary.

"Look Gary, there's no reason Ann would lie, and quite frankly, I hear you guys make sexual comments all day long. We have a sexual harassment policy. Tom crossed the line. Tom's done."

Gary furled his eyebrows and looked down his nose at Sean.

"I know Tom wouldn't say anything like that. It's her word against his. As far as I'm concerned, without a witness, you have no reason to fire him. Just give him a warning if that will make her happy, and that's that." Gary actually was being a bit conciliatory now.

"Gary, you don't run this company. He's got ten minutes to grab his shit and leave, or I'll have a cop arrest him for trespassing."

"A cop?" Gary laughed. "You're going to call a cop you pussy!" Gary smelled Sean's weakness and pounced on it. But I was shocked Gary said that. I think he might have been even shocked that he said it.

"Why don't you just make him leave then?" Gary was out of control. "Go ahead, you physically remove him." He was talking himself into a corner. He wasn't giving Sean an out anymore.

Tom smiled, but I could tell he was a little nervous and unsure. Gary was going to fall on his sword for the dude, but I guess for Gary, especially with a large crowd forming, his dignity was on the line.

Sean looked over at Tom. I couldn't see any nervousness or fear in him. He was as casual and calm as if he were at a bar drinking a beer.

"Tom. You're fired. You leave now, and I'll send you a check for the remainder of the pay period. Time to go."

It was all over. Sean wasn't budging and now Tom had money on the line. Tom started to walk off, but Gary wasn't budging either.

"No fuck that!" Gary was starting to breathe heavy now. You could tell the nervousness in his voice. His adrenaline was pumping. His fight or flight instinct had been set off, and he wasn't thinking straight.

"I'm sick and tired of you slick-ass big city fuckers treating us all like dogs." He looked around trying to drum up some kind of popular, working class support. I looked the other way and checked out Marla's ass.

"You walk around like you're gods. Ever since day one, you think us locals are nothing but uneducated hicks. Let me tell you something, what do you think your parents or grandparents did? Or did your whole family start off rich on the fucking Mayflower? We're the ones making an honest living, earning our small paychecks while you guys fuck around the office, joking, playing games, flirting. You call it networking." He made air quotes. "You call it business lunch. I call it goofing off. That's all it is, goofing off. You get paid what? $100 bucks an hour to chit chat and flirt and fuck around while we're breaking our backs out here for $100 a day? Fuck you! You know what? Fuck you, fuck all you stuck up, big city faggots!" He walked right up to Sean, "And fuck you most of all." He stuck his finger out to jab Sean, but Sean pivoted his body, grabbed Gary's wrist with his right hand and popped his elbow with his left. He kicked Gary's right knee and made Gary do a face plant right into the cement floor. It was all in one smooth, seamless, fluid movement. Gary was on his ass before he knew what happened. Everyone was in shock.

"You're fired too," Sean said glibly as Gary was trying to figure out what had just happened.

If I was Sean, I would have jumped on Gary's back and knocked him out, because there was no way Gary could get up and just walk off with his tail between his legs. Gary was fucked. Sean just punked him. Gary got to his knees and looked over at Sean. There was doubt and uncertainty in his eyes at first, but then like a curtain, rage covered his face as it turned red.

Gary rushed Sean, but Sean once again pivoted and kicked him in the knee sending him sprawled out on the ground again. I could only wish Gary would learn how to fall properly and do a roll or something and land on his feet. Gary was a lumbering mess. I never heard 300 plus pounds of flesh hit a concrete floor before, but I'd never forget it.

Gary got up again. Now, the warehouse guys were getting excited and hooting and hollering for Gary. "Fuck him up man!" "Get up Gary! Get up!" "Go get him Gary!" The management guys were starting to breathe heavy. I don't think they were as good fighters as Sean was and were probably getting worried about being jumped themselves. The women started gasping. "Oh my God!" "No, no, no!" "Stop, no!" People now were running out to the warehouse.

Gary rushed Sean again, but suddenly shifted direction. Sean wasn't expecting that. He must have assumed Gary was stupider than he looked. Just as Sean was about to kick him again, Gary twisted his body and punched Sean right in the chest with an uppercut left. Sean finally looked surprised and stumbled back a few feet. His eyes opened wide.

Gary came back with an overhand right, but Sean ducked it and punched him in the jaw with a right hook. This took Gary back a bit, but it didn't seem to faze him. Gary came back and grabbed Sean. He tried to throw Sean down, but Sean threw an uppercut that bloodied Gary's nose. Gary swung wildly with a right hook, but Sean ducked and grabbed Gary's right leg and twisted and swept Gary's left leg taking him down to the ground. Gary hit the back of his head on the concrete. It sounded like it hurt.

Before Gary could react, Sean was behind Gary's back and put him in a rear naked choke. Gary started gagging. His face turned tomato red. The warehouse guys were yelling, "Pussy!" "You gonna choke him out you pussy!" "Fight like a man!"

A few years back, UFC came out, and there was a guy named Royce Gracie. He took everyone down to the ground and either arm-barred them into submission or choked them out. Ever since, guys have been studying Brazilian Jiu-Jitsu and going to ground grappling. There was nothing wrong with out-grappling a dude and choking him out, but the warehouse guys thought it was just cheap kung-fu shit and didn't really count for winning a fight fair and square.

As Gary was going limp, Sean let up. Gary started wheezing and hacking. His adrenaline was done. He was exhausted. Sean meanwhile was totally fresh.

"You done fat boy?"

The warehouse guys were egging Gary on.

"Fuck you!" Gary got to his feet. He put up his fists like a boxer. His eyes were glassy. He looked like he was going to pass out. They started circling each other. Sean started kicking Gary in the thighs. The kicks looked like they hurt. They sounded like thwack! Each time, Gary lurched to the side. Gary kept wildly swinging at him. Sean then swung wildly at Gary which was odd, but just as Gary ducked down, Sean leapt in the air and kneed Gary right in the chin. Gary's knees buckled. Sean was over Gary now and started going to town on his face. Gary grabbed him, and they were wrestling for a bit. I'm not sure how it happened, but Sean now had Gary's head in a scissor lock with his legs. Then all of a sudden Sean let out a scream.

"Ahhhhhh. You bit me you motherfucker!" I had never heard Sean cuss before. I guess when you get in a fight, we all become working class.

With his head clamped in Sean's legs, Gary had bitten Sean in the leg. Sean then nailed Gary right in the nutsack, and then again, and again, and again, and again, and again. I was saying to myself, "Holy shit!" Dudes were cringing. You could see the fat ripple through Gary's torso.

Gary was in la-la-land. He wasn't unconscious, but he wasn't entirely conscious either.

Sean got up. He checked his leg, and there was a little blood trickling down. I wondered if Gary took a chunk out, but I didn't see any rip in his pants just a patch of blood. A couple years ago, Mike Tyson took a chunk of Evander Holyfield's ear. When I heard about it, I couldn't believe it.

A warehouse guy went over to help Gary, but Gary reacted and kicked the guy in the face and knocked his safety goggles off. The guy screamed and cussed. "Motherfucker! Fuck you Gary! Fuck you!" I thought he was going to start beating on Gary.

Gary was breathing hard, but he didn't know where the fuck he was. They eventually helped him over to the warehouse office where he lay down on the couch looking miserable and pathetic. He was moaning and moaning. I had never heard or seen such a pathetic sight. I couldn't imagine how much agony he was in getting punched in the nutsack so many times. I couldn't imagine how swollen his balls must have been the next morning. I felt so sorry for him. He got his ass handed to him. You couldn't blame Sean. Sean was fighting fair and only hit him in the nuts when he got bit.

I went back to the office. Everyone was in shock. I had seen fights on the street and on UFC before, but I can't imagine how traumatizing it was for the women. A few were shaking and had to be consoled in the break room. The white collar guys were all jumping up and down reenacting the whole fight and patting themselves on the back for showing the warehouse guys who were in charge. It's interesting how in America, at least, guys who go to college tend to be very athletic and muscular, just as much as the guys who don't go to college. If anything, the guys who don't go to college just get fat and lazy while the college educated guys keep working out and lifting weights. I'd imagine in England, the cockney dudes, those crazy soccer fans would totally beat the shit out of the posh Eton boys.

Two things happened after "the fight." First, you never heard a peep out of the warehouse guys again. They never made eye contact with the managers again. A few were even conciliatory and acted all nice and kind. Second, Sean became a legend. There was no question now; he was the alpha dog. Not only did all the guys acknowledge that but even all the managers and Sam. Sam was falling apart feeling useless. Sean had stepped in as the heir apparent and future president. Even I had to acknowledge Sean was alpha over me. I knew now for certain that he could kick my ass, and the last thing I wanted was to wind up like Gary. I sidestepped and avoided Sean. I didn't kiss his ass, but I didn't challenge him either.

Oh, and there was a third thing that happened. The women in the office, shocked and appalled at the unnecessary violence and primitive macho display, all fell head over heels for Sean including Andrea. They became an item, and I seethed with jealousy.

Chapter 7: Playing by the Rules

The managers usually went out for drinks on Friday night at Roxy's, and I knew it, but I was drunk at Brew Bros, a restaurant and club next door. I went over to Roxy's. I was feeling particularly feisty. I went to the bar and ordered a beer and a red bull. Sean was there with Andrea. Mark came up to the bar and greeted me.

"Hey Bill, how's it going."

"Hey Mark. So you guys hang out here?" I already knew they did, and he probably knew that I knew they knew I knew.

"Oh yeah. We just hang out for a few drinks, unwind, you know, end of the week shit."

Mark ordered a cognac.

"You like cognac?" he asked. I felt stupid holding my Amstel Light and Red Bull.

"Oh no, it's a bit much."

"Hey, let me buy you a glass."

"Oh, no, you don't have to."

"No, come on, have a glass with me." He called over the bartender. "How about another one for my buddy."

I really didn't want to get fucked up. I felt like confronting Sean. I didn't want to fight him, but who knew, just in case.

"Good seeing you buddy." Mark shook my hand and didn't invite me over. I slammed the cognac. It must have cost ten bucks or more. It was nice and surprisingly smooth. Didn't taste like the horseshit whiskey's I'd tried before.

I saw Sean see me over here, and he was laughing. He had his arm around Andrea. I was thinking about leaving. Nothing good would come from me confronting him. My job was on the line. But part of me just didn't give a fuck. Someone had to stand up to Sean and put him in his place, and I was thinking I was the only one with the balls and intellect to challenge him. I wasn't looking necessarily to win and act like I owned the place, but I wanted him to know that he wasn't untouchable. I could knock him down a few rungs. He wasn't god.

I looked over at the exit, and it was one of those moments in life where there was a fork in the road, and I could have gone either way. There were bigger, better fish to fry at Brew Bros. What the fuck was I doing chasing a meth head dating my boss? My anger and hatred got the better of me. Even worse, I thought to myself, if I walked away, I was a pussy. Last thing I wanted to deal with was a night full of regret and emotional self-abuse, perhaps the next day, perhaps a week, a month, a lifetime. I was no coward. Pressure built up under my eyes and sinuses at the thought of being a pussy for walking away. I found myself walking toward the group as if outside of my body. My legs were moving, but I wasn't in charge of them.

"Bill!" Sean yelled. He smiled and raised his gay wine glass at me. "How the hell are you doing?"

He seemed so nice and friendly and charming. I almost lowered my defenses.

"Pretty good, just in the neighborhood."

"Reno? That neighborhood?" Everyone at the table laughed, even Andrea. That infuriated me.

"It's a small town," I lobbed back.

"Cheers to that." He clinked Andrea's glass of white wine. She didn't even like to drink with me. She didn't know shit about wine either. She thought Cabernet Sauvignon was a white wine.

There was a brief awkward pause. Nobody at the table was going to go back to talking. They were either purposefully making it awkward for me to stand there, or they were waiting for a cue from Sean like a bunch of sycophant pussies.

"You know, not everyone here is a Podunk redneck. Andrea's from here," I began. Touché.

Sean smiled and looked at the others.

"Who's saying everyone's a Podunk redneck Bill?"

"I don't know. You guys like to make fun of Reno. It has the outdoors. It has Tahoe. It ain't that bad." I couldn't believe myself defending a city I often berated openly.

"It is what it is." Sean looked over at Andrea and kissed her. She giggled like a fucking moron. "It has its local charm." He grabbed her knee, or thigh, I couldn't tell from where I was standing.

He was mocking me. He knew I had dated Andrea. I was livid.

"Well you came here. You could have gone to a big city: San Francisco, New York, Chicago."

"You know what Bill," Sean adjusted himself in his seat. He seemed to be getting irritated with me. "It's a paradigm shift. Opportunity in the big city. That is so yesterday. With the Internet, you can live in a Podunk like Reno, Boise, Idaho, Biloxi, wherever the fuck, and so long as you have access to the Internet, you can make a killing. Small town people crowding to big cities, that was yesterday, that's the Chinese paradigm. That was where all the factory jobs were, but in the Information Age, the jobs are wherever. The factories are in fucking China and Mexico. No more over-crowding, traffic, wasted time commuting, wasted resources, pollution, spreading of diseases. You think animals in industrial farms are sick, just look at humans in big cities. That's the picture of the future my friend." Later I would find out Sean grew up in a small town in Illinois.

I was insulted by him condescendingly lecturing me, although I felt he was right.

"Well, I think big cities will still be relevant with all the corporations taking over, all this consolidation, cartels, trusts, oligopolies, monopolies. Isn't that what your goal for eGo is, merging, selling out?"

"Are you a Communist Bill?"

The table broke the tension with laughter.

"No I'm a libertarian Sean."

"Oh, a free market, anarcho-primitivist, anarcho-Capitalist, Hayekian libertarian." I had no idea what an anarcho-primitivist or anarcho-Capitalist was. I promised myself I'd look it up that night. "So you read Hayek?"

"Yeah, Friedrich von Hayek."

"Friedrich Hayek," he corrected me. "Which book?"

"Just excerpts, his general theses, in textbooks." I was getting flustered. I had underestimated Sean. "What books have you read?"

"Well I'm not a libertarian, and I don't give a shit for them, but if you want to know, I've read *Road to Serfdom* and *The Fatal Conceit*. Have you read Ayn Rand?"

"I – no."

"What's your argument against corporations?"

"Companies have a natural life cycle. They start out small and compete freely, and the most productive, innovative, and efficient thrive while the less efficient go out of business. They sell their assets, free up resources, it's an efficient process. But then when you're left with several, they start to engage in illegal and unfair market practices. Corporate lobbyists ensure that anti-trust laws are not enforced and they don't prosecute unfair market practices, or they just hire so many lawyers, cases get tied up for years. With mergers, you eventually get oligopoly or monopoly. Efficiency, innovation, productivity go down. Quality goes down. Price goes up. Profit goes up. It just becomes a leach on the efficiency of society. On top of that, with control of the President and his federal agencies, they're free to poison us."

"Excellent." He raised his eyebrows at the group. I was proud of myself. I took a deep breath.

"But what if nobody is playing by free market rules to begin with? Why restrict only a few to the rules while letting others break the rules?"

"What do you mean? Who's breaking the rules besides corporations?"

"Well, OPEC, national tariffs, trade restrictions, taxes, fees, unions, minimum wage, subsidized housing, rent control, collective bargaining, international banks, Communist countries, China, government subsidies of key industries, Japan, the EU, protectionism. Why is it the Communists and unions can break free market rules but the American corporations can't?"

"Well, I'm an advocate for all these players following the rules."

"Okay, but in what fantasy world do you see OPEC dissolving, Communist China going democratic, the EU not negotiating trade collectively, countries eliminating all tariffs and trade restrictions, and unions breaking up? This is like saying, oh, I believe in a society where cars run on water and cost a dollar. That's a goal, a fantasy; it's not an ideology, a way to run society. That's like saying, I'd love a world without nuclear bombs, I'll be the first to get rid of mine, anyone else want to join me?"

"Well, we can strive towards a goal."

"Well, yes, and isn't that what Communism is about. How do you force all these players to play by the rules? Autocratic tyranny might work, but then you have the even worse problem of autocratic tyranny. So, tell me, what instrument or mechanism is going to make everyone play by the rules all at once at 5 o'clock this Sunday afternoon?"

"So just because everyone else is not engaging in free market rules, we don't? Is that your logic?"

"Tell you what Bill. You be the first to play by the rules and see how far that gets you. You're an idealist, and while I respect that, you're also a daydreamer and you live in this alternate universe utopia where everyone plays fair. Didn't you learn in college or at least high school that we don't live in a fantasy world? It's dog eat dog out there. You play rough or you don't get the bone." He squeezed Andrea for emphasis.

"Your whole concept of the world is fucked up." I came back. "So you're a Monetarist, a Keynesian? You like the government and the Feds interfering with the free market? You like the fact that the Federal Reserve is nothing but a cartel of banks charging everyone including the government interest for printing money they don't even own? How fucked up is that? The banks are basically taxing the people, and then government taxes the people even more with payroll taxes that are regressive taxes. And don't get me started on credit cards and VISA and the tax on every transaction, what is it a 2 percent fee? Every single credit card transaction, why can't there be a no fee, non-profit or government credit card processing company?"

Sean stood up. I thought he was going to punch me. He grabbed my arm, but in a nice way. He turned back, "Excuse me guys, this will take a few minutes."

"Let's have a little private chat here Bill." He took me to another part of Roxy. I considered telling him not to touch me and fuck off, but it was just weird how I couldn't. Sean made it seem natural to follow him. He was gentle in a forceful way, and I know that sounded gay, but it was the best way of describing it.

"I'll give you a little secret Bill. We all know this. It's not a conspiracy. It's reality. You're a real hero for the working and middle class. What do you want 90% of all Americans in the middle class? You want 90% of all people in the world in the middle class?"

"Why not?"

"Are you serious? Five and half billion or so people in the middle class? Five and half billion cars? You know what middle class people do Bill? They consume. They consume like pigs. Sure the upper class consumes more per family, but there are hardly as many of them. Middle class people are fat pigs. At least poor people aren't wasteful. How many middle class people do you know who have a TV for every bedroom, more than one car, a house with unused rooms, and boy they eat like pigs too. The world's resources may last a few thousand more years, but five and half billion pigs and I bet you they'd all be done in a few decades. Well, who gets to decide who's rich and who's poor? You're lucky you're in America, because you're the only one who decides. You don't need to study art or music. You don't need to buy a new car. You don't need to buy a house right away. You don't need to buy fancy clothes or shoes. You can study hard, work your ass off, save your money, start your own business and join the upper class. You just don't get it. This world just can't handle a big middle class. But it's not unfair. You had a shot just like everyone else. You graduated from Stanford. It's not like you didn't have the brains."

"Well, I'd rather live with integrity and dignity than without."

Sean looked away and then came back, "You drive an old beat up Buick Regal. You used to live in a weekly motel. You graduated from Stanford somehow, but you haven't done anything with your life, and you started working for eGo as an $8 dollar an hour data entry clerk. Is that dignified? Look, I admire you for graduating from Stanford. Obviously, you're a smart dude. But somewhere along the way, someone fed you a line of bullshit about how the world is, and you've been pissed off ever since, that it isn't as perfect as you want it to be. Maybe it was literature class, because as I remember, every fucking writer is a whiner who never gets the girl and sits around bitching and prattling on about injustices, because he's a gimp, a short wimp, or mentally unstable. So instead of playing the game as it's being played, you quit, you sat out. You decided to sit on the sidelines and mock, belittle, and criticize all the players. Meanwhile, you ran out of money and started living like a bum. I don't blame you for being angry, but buddy, your anger is misplaced. We're not the problem Bill. We're playing the same game everyone else is playing. You need to start looking at yourself for a change and ask yourself, are you happy sitting this game out and being a bum, or do you want to get in the game and fuck a cheerleader once in a while? There's nothing wrong with shrinking the middle class. They're pigs. They don't invest in technology. They don't create companies. They consume and spend. Fucking bourgeois pigs! I'll agree with Karl Marx on that. I love the proletariat too. I think everyone except a few rich folk should be proletariat. How much was the Soviet Union consuming and wasting with all those poor fucks? Not hardly as much as Americans."

"I gotta pee." Sean not only handed me my ass, in the same fashion he handed Gary his ass, but unlike with Gary, Sean gave me an out. He wasn't mocking me or insulting me. He gave me an out. I was humbled. Everything he said made sense, and over the next few days, as I thought about it more and more, it made more and more sense. I was a rebel with a stupid cause. I was the cause of my own ruin. It was all me all along. I owed Sean the most important revelation and concept of my life, responsibility.

Sean soon broke up with Andrea and started dating an even hotter woman he picked up at Roxy. I even considered that as some peace offering to me. Andrea was devastated. I would have consoled her, but last thing I wanted to do was look like I wanted scraps. I was also angry at Andrea. I could care less. The bitch got exactly what she deserved. She OD'ed on drugs and went to the hospital and never returned to eGo. eGo was for winners. Andrea was a loser.

Chapter 8: Delusion

Over the next few weeks, Sean talked to me more, but this time around as a sort of mentor. We even went to the gym together. I hadn't worked out since high school. He put me to shame. His body was rock solid. He didn't break a sweat as I grunted and dripped through a weight circuit doing half the weight he was lifting. I was so delusional to even think I could possibly beat him in a fight. He was fucking benching 260 pounds. I could barely lift 140. He was a man. Next to him, I felt like a boy. One night, we went to a yoga room, and he taught me a few boxing and grappling moves. I told him I wanted to learn what he did to Gary. We put on some boxing gloves, and I swear, every time I came in with a hook, he'd jab me straight into my face and smear my sweat all over my face. When I jabbed, he ducked and came in with a hook, not full force, but popping my ribs making me know with full force, it would do damage, maybe crack a rib or two. Then he kept popping me with jabs, and at one point, with sweat getting in my eyes, I was panic-stricken. I was getting my ass kicked. Would Sean let up on me? Was he teaching me a lesson? Was he fucking beating the shit out of me? Would I go to work the next day with black eyes, and he would tell them all he beat the shit out of me for fun? I kept laughing and smiling it off, but I was really fucking worried. Pressure was building up under my eyes. I didn't want to cry, but I couldn't fucking take it out on him. Then I said, "Maybe we should do some grappling. I'm better with grappling." With all the sweat around my eyes and hyperventilating, maybe I was crying. Sean slapped me on the back reassuringly.

So we took off the gloves and grappled. I didn't know what the fuck I was doing. I remember wrestling from junior high school, and I was quick. I could take out guys 20, 40 pounds heavier than me. But I'd go in for his legs to take him down, and he'd just spread his legs out and shove my head down. I started to realize just how much stronger he was than me. He was throwing me around like a rag doll. Every time I'd try to move him, he'd grab my arm, twist me this way, that way, I'd lose balance, my leg would be in an awkward place, and he'd just flip me or mount me. But he gave me pointers. *Move your arm here. Spread your legs there. Grab my wrist. Don't let me get under hooks. Jam your elbow into my thigh. Don't give me any space. Breathe!*

I couldn't believe how tiring grappling was. Of course, I was probably holding my breath a lot. I could smell the blood vessels in my lungs. When we took a break, I lay on my back, and the room was spinning, and I was seeing stars. It wasn't like in the cartoons, but pin pricks of light. I thought I was going to pass out. Sean wasn't even breaking a sweat. He then showed me how to choke someone out. He put a rear naked on me, and I swear my head was going to explode. I must have looked like a tomato. I tapped out immediately. I put a rear naked on him, and his neck muscles just tightened, and I squeezed and squeezed and squeezed. He kept giving me tips. I couldn't choke him out. I felt useless. I started to wonder. Was he trying to help me, or was he like showing me just how badass he was. You know, if you meet some dude who wants to fight you, you don't just fight him. You make friends, take him out to your gym, see what he's got, and then school him. He realizes what a fool he was for even thinking about fighting you. It was humiliating. I was on my back, semi-conscious. I had worked my ass out before in sports, but I had never been so close to passing out in my life. Sean helped me to my feet although I would have much preferred to stay on the ground.

"Good job man!" he slapped my ass. It felt gay. I would never slap a dude's ass. "Grab a shower." I panicked. The showers were communal. The last thing I was going to do was see Sean naked or have him see me naked, how gay was this?

"Hey, I think I'll grab a protein shake out front and cool down." Save.

Every inch of my body ached the next day. I swore from that day forward, I'd exercise regularly, learn martial arts, and get some of my dignity back.

My next lesson came by way of hanging out one night when I told him about my interest in philosophy.

"So what do you write about?" Sean asked.

"I write novels and non-fiction."

"What kind of non-fiction?"

"Psychology and philosophy, society, human nature."

"Okay, what about?"

"Everything. Life. The meaning of life, humanity."

"Jesus that's vague. You'll have to send me the manuscript one of these days. What's your thesis statement?"

"Well, it's about the Industrial Age and how it's dehumanized man, how it's stripped us of our humanity. It boils us down to instincts, individual and social. A lot of people forget that we are social creatures, and modern corporate Capitalism has taken away our social values and replaced it with this twisted contract. You glorify yourself, you cloak yourself in materialism, consumerism, fashion, trendiness, and only then can you fit in, only then can you get social rewards: attention, belonging, identity, love. And if you don't buy into all this crap, you get the social punishments of loneliness, embarrassment, humiliation, scorn, irrelevance. People who don't look right, dress right, make enough money, own the right car, go to the right restaurant, hang out at the right scene, they're losers, they're inconsequential, they're invisible. But people don't realize, you do all these things to achieve individual goals: glamour, fame, fortune, but you become self-infatuated, and nobody wants to hang out with you. So you're going in the wrong direction not the right direction. All you need to fit in and have friends and find love is to practice your social skills. You can't do that shopping, fixating on the media, keeping up with trends, joining in on the scorn of outcasts."

"That's pretty fucking heavy dude. You heard of the Unabomber?"

"Yeah. What does that have anything to do with it?"

"He wrote a manifesto blaming industrialism for the decline of humanity."

"Yeah, well, he was nuts."

"No, it's a blame game. You don't have to play if you don't want to. You know, they did psychological experiments on him in college? You know all those old psyc experiments: the Milgram Experiment, the Stanford Prison Experiment, Asch Conformity Experiment, all that shit?"

"Yeah, Psyc 101." I hadn't heard of the Asch one but looked it up later and remembered it.

"They were all mind-fucking experiments, and they fucked with Ted Kaczynski's mind and questioned his whole identity and belief system, and it traumatized him. Maybe it wasn't the main cause that he went nuts, but it definitely contributed to it. You know the US military funded most of the early studies in psychology? They were scared of all the brainwashing shit going on in the Soviet Union and China. They wanted to figure that shit out themselves and just like in the space race, they wanted to outdo the Soviets. Well they did. It was the Psyc race dude, people don't know that. But then you got this extrapolation into advertising and controlling consumer minds. They also invented a lot of the drugs we now use recreationally. They say they stopped the experiments, but I think bullshit."

I was blown away that he knew so much about psychology for a Finance nerd. He seemed to be pretty well read. I had only read a few self-help books since college.

"So what's the meaning of life?" he asked.

"We make it up. We serve our individual and social instincts. We create civilization with its contracts, so we serve civilization's interests, and in return, it's supposed to take care of our individual and social needs and protect us from threats."

"Nothing more than that? Instincts? Evolution? No God? No spirits? No afterlife? No soul?"

"None of that has been proven."

"Has the Big Bang been proven? Has gravity been proven? We don't even know what gravity is. We don't know what space is or time. Space isn't empty. It isn't a vacuum. You ever study quantum physics?"

"Um, relativity?"

"No, quantum physics. It's about reality. It's about reality being potentialities and existing only within the context of a conscious mind. You can only go so far with psychology and philosophy before you figure it all out or just go around in rhetorical circles and become a sophist. You have to start getting into quantum physics, because that's where all the mind-bending, mind-fucking things come. Meaning of life? Truth? Morality? Freewill? Humanity? Fuck all that. Boring. Already defined. Fuck humanity. Why are we so special? We're mutated primates. There's no reason we should preserve humanity outside the selfish reason we're born with instincts that make us feel we're important enough to preserve. We're designed to fuck, eat, hunt, and crap. We're not designed to understand the cosmos, other dimensions, other universes, other realities. You're stuck in the Classical World of Newtonian Physics my friend, conservation, closed systems. Open your mind up. You're stuck with Nietzsche in his gimpy hell, going around in circles hating life. I'm not saying become a Christian or anything, but your philosophy is constricting you man. It's justifying and dignifying your misery, but it's also enfeebling you. My philosophy is simple. We're stupid, fucking, selfish, greedy, faulty, mutated primates, and before a greater being catches on to us and our destructive, sick ways and wipes us all out or mutates us into something more like them, we might as well fucking enjoy our time in the sun. Fulfill all your individual and social needs. I'm not saying just short-term, selfish gratification, but all your social needs: love, affirmation, belonging, identity. No excuses. Just no excuses. Mould your philosophy around your needs not your fears. Fuck Nietzsche, what has he done for you lately? Nietzsche is a nerd. He's an opiate for all the nerds who can't get laid and enjoy life. Nietzsche is dead."

"I'm not totally into Nietzsche, but I get your point."

"He was right about everything being a delusion: morality, freewill, but he was just as deluded for thinking that humanity was special, that we could be supermen. Why? Who the fuck cares? Being the best you can be? That's delusional, why not be a lamo fuckwit? Why not be a homicidal nutsack? You just pick your delusions, whatever serves you.

The one thing we do know, that gives life meaning, that has been with us for 200 thousand years and animals forever are our two basic instincts: desires and fears. The most fundamental reason we move, why cells move, why amoeba move, why humans move, is to recoil from a threat or seek out something we desire. Otherwise movement is just wasted energy. But humans have one more thing, the conscious mind, and that's where we got it all fucked up. See, we think we can artificially quench all our desires and eliminate our threats, but that's not what we're designed for, and we will rebel, at least unconsciously against it. Spoiled kids who get everything they desire, they rebel by being little drama queens. Spoiled princes turn into tyrannical kings who send their people to war. When society has too much order and security, they also rebel and create unrest, so their leaders have to terrorize them occasionally with war, persecution, or ritualized sacrifices of citizens. When a human has everything he desires and no threats, he becomes paranoid, disturbed, because that's not natural. His threat avoidance system needs to be exercised, so he manufactures threats just to practice recoiling from them. He sabotages his food supply, just to practice starving and hunger. Isn't that what Buddha did after all? Abundance and total security is not natural, and it drove him nuts, so he left it all.

Look at city planning. Well planned cities are ugly bastions of grids and superhighways, but humans want and crave disorder, curved roads, mysterious neighborhoods, non-Euclidean natural structure. Fact is, we don't like too much order and security, and we actually crave a little terror. That's why when you give someone everything, they still destroy, they get addictions, they become perverse and reckless. If there is a God, he was right to create the devil and evil, because we need that. Without the devil and evil, we would infuse evil into our pleasures, pervert eating, recreation, sex, love, friendships. You can't be all good if you don't know what evil is, and you can't know evil without bringing about its existence. You think sometime in the future, we can get rid of this weird genetic instinct of fear after eliminating all our threats, but truth is, even if we knew how, we shouldn't. It's half of who we are."

"It almost sounds like you're rationalizing evil and immorality."

"I'm not saying endorse the truly heinous things like genocide or torture which is actually perverted evil, but I'm saying every now and then, it's okay to be a dick. Endorse the fun bad things, the small pure evils, the small injustices, the bad behavior, the fighting, the small moral infractions so you don't get so morally uptight that you wind up perverting good and then shit out a horrendous, perverted huge evil like molesting children. We try too hard to eliminate our threats and ensure our security, but if we just allowed some threats through and a certain level of insecurity, that's natural, that gives us balance. It's like what they discovered about forest fires, you let some fires burn. If you eliminate all the fires, the forest floor gets littered with flammable debris so it accumulates into a super-destructive forest fire. We have to follow nature. We don't have the expertise of millions of years of evolution."

After reading *A Brief History of Time*, I came to the sober conclusion that I really had no idea what the fuck I was talking about. I was a fraud. Sean was so much smarter than me. I thought of myself as this great philosopher who would change the world, write that indispensable Philosophy 101 book. I thought nobody knew what I knew. Sean knew everything and more. How could I have been so deluded? Was I really like Ted Kaczynski? I reread my philosophy manuscript and realized perhaps I was. I was supposed to be an expert on psychology and philosophy, and I hadn't even read any psychology and philosophy books after college. I hated Sean. He did it for fun, and he was better at it than me. He was like some kind of Mozart, and I was Salieri. As much as I hated him, I admired him, and I aspired to be more like him. So long as I was learning and growing because of him, I was grateful to him. Because of him, I started to read books again, shitloads of books, more than I had ever read in high school or college combined.

"So you graduated from Stanford with a degree in Economics," Sean asked me one day at work. "You went straight from that to data entry. What happened?"

"The economy."

"Okay, but even in a shitty economy, you're taking the bottom of the bottom. There's still better jobs out there. Hell, bartenders make more than data entry clerks."

"I don't know I guess I never really tried hard to look."

"Did you make any contacts in college? Were you in a fraternity?"

"No, I hated frats."

"Okay, well, that's what frats are for, getting contacts, networking. You wanted to go into business, but you didn't do any networking?"

"Well, I thought I wanted to go into business, but I guess I lost interest after taking Accounting and Finance."

"Yeah, but you got a degree in Economics. You can't possibly tell me Economics is easier than Accounting and Finance. I aced Accounting and Finance and struggled through Economics. There's no Calculus in Accounting and Finance. A fucking 8th grader could ace Accounting and Finance."

"Well, I guess it just wasn't for me, following all those rules and stuff."

"But there are rules in Economics, there are rules in everything. There are rules in baseball. You don't have to be an expert, just pass the damn test, get a B or C even and you're fine."

"I know, but I guess I just lost all motivation. I just couldn't pick up the textbooks for the life of me. Maybe I just burned out."

"Well, then if you're not going to be a technical genius, if you want to succeed in business, you better as shit be a social networking genius. Bill, there are two types of people in business. There are the technical dudes, the nerds, who are great in math and science and the mathematical side of business like financial analysis and accounting. They get ahead by simply being good at what they do. But there's also the social geniuses, the ones who make all the deals, sell the product, open businesses, get investors excited, find investors, find buyers. They have to know some basic accounting and finance, but shit, they can get C's in that and excel even become CEO's. You were neither."

"Yeah, but I also lost interest in going into business. So what was left for me? I got a degree in Economics and no craft, no technical skill."

"Look Bill, back in the Paleolithic Age the physically strong and those with the greatest endurance, they survived and reproduced. In the Neolithic Age with agriculture and civilization, the greatest threats are not wild animals or starvation but other humans. Those who survive and reproduce are those who excel at social skills, because the higher up the social ladder you climb, the safer you are from ritualized sacrifices, being sent off to war, living on the periphery of the city and being vulnerable to bandits and attack. Whether business or any other human enterprise Bill, you need social skills or you die. If you want a job, you needed to network. I mean, even if you didn't want to join a fraternity, the apex of the social ladder in college, you still could have joined clubs, societies, something, anything. That's how you find jobs, that's how you get ahead, get your foot in the door. Did you ask any of your professors if they knew of any jobs you could apply for? Did you have friends with parents looking for new hires? Did you have classmates who may have known about job openings?"

"Yeah, I guess I wasn't thinking. I pretty much kept to myself. I did apply for a few jobs, but nothing happened."

"Well, now it's different Bill. Now you know me, and you know what the greatest thing about knowing me is Bill? No, it's not that I'm such a great guy Bill; it's the plain and simple fact that I have a network of over ten thousand contacts. I joined a fraternity, clubs, hung out with my professors, spent summers with my friends and got to know their families, their families' businesses, their families' friends and business contacts, heck I wound up working for my friend's family's friend's business. I did the networking, and just by strange, weird luck, you entered my network, and now, you have access to all of that. You ever need a job, I can ask my frat buddies, dudes in my frat all over the country, my friends, my family, my friends' families' friends. Do you understand me Bill? Networking is not about meeting people, it's about meeting the networks they're attached to. You network with a hundred nerds; your network perhaps only doubles. You network with a hundred strong networkers, and your network grows exponentially."

"Well, I got no one in my network, so why did you network with me?"

He laughed.

"Bill, did you ever notice just how many people in this company know you? I know all the new folks, the new management team, but you know everyone who worked here before we came. You don't stay to yourself here. I see you going off talking to guys in the warehouse, customer service, marketing, sales, jumping all over the place. Through you, I make contact with all of them. Do you get that?"

"Huh, I guess I never realized that I was networking here."

"Yeah, and you have the technical skills to be the best one at your job, and that's also why you were promoted to head your department. You really do have everything it takes to get ahead Bill, but you keep yourself back by your attitude, your hang-ups, your distrust of authority. You fucked up in college, but you have what it takes to make up for it all now. Do you get that Bill? Of all the people in this company, you have the greatest potential of them all, both on the technical and networking side."

In hindsight, I considered the possibility Sean was just blowing smoke up my ass to get my loyalty and trust, but never in my life had anyone, ever, ever told me that I had potential, that I was good at something, that I had ability. Every great accomplishment I had, my parents either ignored or downplayed. I won skiing competitions, even made it to the Junior Olympic training camp, and even after getting into Stanford, my parents never, ever told me they were proud or impressed. "Yeah, but how many kids do they accept into that Olympic training camp? And it's not the Senior training camp, it's probably just some big camp to motivate kids like some NBA kid's camp. And you didn't get into the Stanford Business School. What are you going to do with an Economics degree? Stanford Business School is where you should have gotten in."

Sean could have been all playing me to be on my side, but at least he had something positive and encouraging to say. I was totally sold on him. He had my loyalty. I started really enjoying coming into work and felt I was making a really big contribution. I "networked" even more at work, sensing somehow that he was right. I had both the technical and networking skills to really get ahead in life.

I started looking back at my parents and realized just how anti-social they were. They couldn't build up and encourage someone or get someone's loyalty if their lives depended on it. My father-in-law was virtually autistic, and my mother was so negative and hateful and paranoid and mistrustful of people that she never let anyone get close to her. Neither of them had any friends. They were loners, anti-social losers. They were nerds, but even worse, they didn't even have any technical abilities. I was becoming just like them, but they always thought that my only chance of getting ahead was excelling in school, going to Stanford, becoming a mega-nerd genius and getting by on my technical skills not my social skills. Perhaps my rebellion was against this. I had friends. I had better social skills than them. I could get by on both my technical and social skills. They didn't understand this. For them, they just saw me as a nerd genius or a total loser, but I could strike that balance between both technical and social aptitude. I didn't want to blame my previous failures on them, but perhaps they had a lot to do with it. The reason I hated Accounting and Finance so much was that they were not social sciences. They were not about people. I was interested in people after all. I was captivated by the psychology of people, by the social dynamics, by the relationships. I wanted to be social. I didn't want to be just a nerd. I needed to leave them in my past and move forward with Sean. I bet Sean's parents were socially gifted. I bet he had a lot of friends growing up. He had all the advantages, and that's why he was where he was. I probably would never end up there, but with Sean's help, perhaps, I'd get a lot closer than I would have ever imagined without him.

My next lesson was on women. I was never really good at hitting on women. I was unfortunately shy around women, although I could be very gregarious and outgoing around guys. It was probably a family thing growing up with a messed up and domineering mother. He told me that I was too much of a feminist and how treating women as equals in the workplace was fine, but if I tried to treat them like that outside of work, they would lose respect for me.

"See Bill, your problem is that women think of you as the nice guy in the office. You're nice. You're funny. You make women laugh, but they don't take you seriously. You sometimes try too hard. You have to be the asshole, the alpha. Don't let them tease you and get away with it. Bring them down a notch. Question their hair, their style. They may act like they resent it, and they do, in fact, but they won't resent you. They'll respect you. They'll go, man, that Bill, he's an asshole, but he's also kind of sexy. Right now, they're all like, man, that Bill is a kind, gentle, nice guy, and I would never sleep with him. But don't get me wrong, I don't mean be a total dick. There's a fine line. Some guys are dicks, because they're immature and think abusing women is fun, and they get women, but the women they get have low self-esteem and are low class full of tats. Know what tats are? Emotional scars. Stay away from them. They probably also have diseases and some sort of addiction or mental problem."

I noted that half the women in Reno have tats. I thought of Andrea and Marla.

"You can have fun with them, but you don't want them around for long, because you don't get a reputation as a player with them, you get a reputation as a bottom feeder. Now, let me ask you, what in your mind is an ideal woman?"

I thought to myself for a little.

"Physically," he added. "Don't give me this bullshit about caring, loving, nurturing, good conversationalist crap."

"I guess, well, I don't really go for any race, but you know, like ideally, I guess some supermodel right, like blonde, 5'8", slim, young, early 20's."

"How tall are you?"

"I, I'm like 5'9"."

Sean looked at me directly in the eyes.

"Okay, look, everyone wants to drive a Bentley or Ferrari right. Every boy grows up dreaming, and every boy grows up dreaming of dating a supermodel, but here's the reality check dude. Unless you're a multi-millionaire, that ain't happening. Look, I don't want to be mean or anything, but the woman you just described isn't looking for you. She's looking for 6 feet plus, $100K plus a year. Look, you're a decent, good looking guy, don't get me wrong, but you're not a stud. When you walk into a nightclub, if I asked you to pick out all the studs, would you pick yourself? When you walk into a bar or nightclub, do you see women checking you out? Okay, once in a blue moon, you may get that supermodel or almost supermodel. I mean, you had Andrea for a while right, but they're all messed up somehow. Bill, you have to shoot lower. There's no other way I can tell you, man, you have to shoot lower. I'm not saying fat and ugly, but what about short, what about 5 feet to 5'5" you ever thought about that?"

"Yeah, I, I guess. You know I guess I have been wasting a lot of my time on tall women." Marla was like 5'10", Andrea was 5'9", and Carey was 5'8". Jesus, Sean was right. Why was I stuck on women as tall as me?

"Okay, great. So that's a starting point. Shorter women and perhaps a little chubby. Dude, the average American woman is overweight. You don't want obese, but you have to face reality. Chances are you're going to end up with an overweight woman."

I didn't like where this was going, but Sean just seemed to know everything about everything. I had three awful reality checks to deal with now. 1. Sean could easily kick my ass. He was twice as fit and strong as I was, and he also knew martial arts. 2. Sean was probably twice as smart as I was, not only in finances and economics but also psychology and philosophy. 3. Sean was a stud, and I was not. Almost every straight woman would consider Sean a hunk. I would guess only 10% of them would look at me that way if that. This was really sucking. Why couldn't I be Sean? Why couldn't I be Sean in a different life? Sean was everything I wanted to be. I felt so inadequate next to him. I used to think I was so much better than people like Sean. I used to think of them as stupid, brainwashed, superficial, weak. I was deluded. How could I be so deluded? I thought I was a tough guy without studying boxing or martial arts, and people like Sean would kick my ass. I thought I was smart without studying anything beyond college, and people like Sean could school me on everything. I thought I was an attractive dude, but people like Sean probably slept with a hundred more women than I ever had. They're just better than me. How can you live with yourself knowing that people like Sean are just all around better than you?

"Okay, so how many women do you hit on a week?"

"A week?" I laughed.

"Okay a month."

"Fuck, I don't know, like three or four." I was exaggerating.

"Christ! Look, I think I know what's going on. You're a thinker Bill. I notice, like, in every meeting, you'll be sitting there thinking like crazy, and I'm a thinker too, but here's the deal. There's a time to think, and there's a time to execute. See, unfortunately, society's churning out all these dumb, executing high school grads and smart but impotent, over-analytical college grads. You have to be both. When it's time to execute, you execute. Hitting on women is an act of instinct. When you approach a woman, your mind must be blank. It must be clear. You can't be thinking of what you're going to say. It's like an artist or writer. You're a writer right. You don't sit there thinking about how to fill up a blank page. You just do it. You don't squeeze it out, you release, and it comes out." Loved the shitting analogy.

"So you approach a woman, and she looks at you, and I promise you, you will instinctively say something. Now, it doesn't have to be the smartest thing in the world. It just shouldn't be a cliché, sexual, religious, or political. But how do you talk to guys at bars? You don't walk up and go, 'Hey buddy, how's it going. Can I buy you a drink? I like your jacket.' No, you go, 'Wow, did you see that home run? Hey, there was some awful accident out there. Is that the wine menu? Can I check it out? You know anything good on there?' Just casual, right? She CAN'T blow you off. Women are trained not to be mean, UNLESS, UNLESS you make it obvious you're hitting on her. I guarantee you to God, if you ask a woman to pass you the wine menu, she will never say, "buzz off."

It all made sense to me. I guess my approach was always a bit too obvious and direct.

"Hey, look," he continued, "I gotta come clean with you okay. When I was going out with Andrea, she told me about you. She liked you a lot, but I'm telling you, she thought of you as a nice guy. I don't want to embarrass you or anything, but you sent her poems and flowers. That's super romantic." I think my face was turning red. I started to wonder whether he was being a good friend giving advice or a condescending ass, or perhaps both. "But those days are gone dude. Women don't respect that shit. Maybe for Valentine's Day and your anniversary but not up front.

So let's start out with your appearance. I don't want to turn you into a fancy boy, but honestly, you dress working class. You go out with gangster jeans and t-shirts or long sleeve t's and some military looking jacket with frayed cuffs. Dude, women don't take that seriously. You look like you're a homeless vet. If you're going out with the guys, going to work on your car, fine, but you're a white collar now dude."

Sean actually gave me a promotion and raise, one reason why I was letting him talk to me like this.

"Now, I notice suits aren't big in Reno, but you can wear a sport jacket and jeans to nicer restaurants and bars. Now, again, don't take this the wrong way Bill, that, that thing on your face, that caterpillar crawling over your mouth. I don't know what's going on there. Moustaches went out with the Village People. Shave it all off Bill, seriously."

That night as I shaved off my scraggily moustache completely, I couldn't help but realize what an insular, deluded world I had lived in.

"What cologne do you wear?"

"*Obsession* by Calvin Klein." I thought he would approve.

"Lose it, what are you a kid in the 80's?" Fuck. "The number one selling cologne is Aqua de Gio. You know why? Because it smells like fucking flowers. The musk comes later, but women don't like musk upfront, it's too overwhelming. Plus, you know what's an even better scent on a man? The scent of another woman and women wear floral shit."

"If they're lesbians…"

"No, you don't get it. A dude that already has a woman is more attractive to a woman than some loner dude who's single. They're thinking, you already got what it takes to get one woman, it intrigues them. Try wearing a wedding ring one night, and go around hitting on women. Women love that shit, cheating whores."

He looked at my watch.

"What the fuck is that?"

"It's a Casio Databank."

"Fuck!" His eyes rolled. "What are you a fucking college nerd?"

"It holds phone numbers."

"SHIT dude!" I was only being facetious with him sort of. "You're not going to get laid with a fucking digital watch. Now, you don't need a Rolex which is not only overvalued but stinks of working class turned nouveau riche, but get a Seiko, Bulova, Citizen, something more yuppie at least. Don't get Invicta, pretty watches, but cheap and not reliable. Spend at least $200, it'll be worth it."

"I can't read hands on a clock."

He wasn't amused.

"What are you wearing?" I asked.

"IWC Chronograph solid gold."

"How much is it?"

"Ten grand."

"Fuckin-a! That's more than my car."

"No shit. And oh, by the way, you have a company car now. Lose your ghetto-mobile essay. We got deals on 99 Mercury Grand Marquis. It's not exactly a pussy wagon, but it's better than your old boat, a pick-up, or a fucking Honda Civic."

"Cool." Dude just bought a 2000 BMW E39 M5 with a 4.9 Liter V8. THAT was a pussy wagon.

He checked out my shoes and lifted my jeans up.

"Doc Martens," I said.

"Are you in a fucking punk band? Did you not notice the punk movement dying in the late 80's?"

"There's a small revival in America."

"Dress shoes."

"I like boots."

"Dress shoes, black socks." He looked at my socks, "Fucking grey socks? Seriously? Whether you like it or not, women check out your ass, your watch, and your shoes first. And teeth." He looked straight at me. "Smile." I didn't smile but showed him my teeth.

"Not bad, they're straight at least. But a bit stained. Bleach them professionally. No home kit, get them bleached. Now your hair. Let me guess, you get it cut at SuperCuts."

"No, I go to GreatClips."

"Go to Metro Salon downtown, they charge $30."

"Shit."

He rolled his eyes. "You can afford it now! Ask for a Brad Pitt. You got a Tom Cruise, wrong decade. And this is Reno. $30 is cheap. Get back to me next week, when you have new cologne, new shoes, new watch, sport jacket, new hair style, and we're going out. If I don't get you laid after two nights out, I'll pay you $500."

"Bullshit."

We shook on it.

Sean gave me $500 but I also blew a paycheck, but I looked in the mirror before going out, and it was weird. I never seemed to have the self-confidence or self-esteem to pull this off. I realized that I purposefully made myself look even worse than I was. I really dressed down. I seemed to be looking for a woman of substance, who wasn't into image like myself, but then why was I hitting on supermodels? I was a fucking idiot. Not to sound weird, but I looked good, and I never felt more confident in my life. I was transformed.

I drove over to Sean's. He was renting a large house in the Southwest outside the McCarran Loop. I never knew any single people who rented houses, but I guess if you have the money, why live in a cramped one-bedroom apartment when you can live in a nice four-bedroom house with a garage and backyard. It looked so empty inside with only me and him.

He wanted to talk to me first and prep me, but as it turned out, he took out a vial of white powder. I had never taken cocaine before. I felt awkward. I considered saying, 'no thank you,' but I also had really wanted to try it just to see what it was like. I never worried about getting addicted. I had taken some really good painkillers in high school and never got addicted to them. He cut up straws and gave me one.

"I thought you were supposed to roll up a dollar or something?" I said, trying to act like I knew something.

"Fuck that shit man! You know how many fucking germs are on currency. More than shopping carts, door handles, probably even more than toilet seats. Fucking homeless people touch that shit, and you ever seen them wash their hands. Fucking children, mothers who wipe their asses, scumbags, fuck that man, grow the fuck up."

He cut up some lines on a mirror, and I found myself awkwardly looking up my nostril. I wasn't sure whether to press one nostril close or stick my finger up it. I stuck my finger up it, and looking back on that, I'm embarrassed for myself, but I was a newbie. I couldn't deceive him into thinking I had done it before. I told him it was my first time.

"Okay, well just do two lines. They're fatties. It's probably less than a quarter of a gram. The shit you get in Reno sucks, so it won't knock you on your ass. It'll just give you a good buzz. I don't know how many fucking times it gets cut up between Columbia, San Francisco, and Reno. See, the problem with booze is that it slows you down. You start slurring your words, your eyes get droopy, women know you're drunk, and they hate that. Because if you're drunk, then it means you might have beer goggles on, and so the only reason you're hitting on them is because you think they're hotter than they really are. I snort to keep myself up all night long. I'm mellow, and I'm quick. I can think around any woman. I can beat any excuse or put down or sarcastic remark. You see, it's not about just being charming and charismatic; it's also about being mellow, alert, and persistent. Never get offended. Never quit. Unless, of course, she's being a total bitch, then it's just not worth it."

He cut up and took a few lines. He took deep breaths. It smelled like ammonia. "Rub some on your gums." I rubbed a little on my gums.

"Numb."

"Yeah, that's how you tell it's the real thing, but then again some douches cut their shit up with lidocaine."

He brought out a couple Stella's and we cheered. I didn't feel it that much. I just felt a little buzz like drinking an espresso.

We hit Foley's across the Peppermill. I always thought it was a dive bar, but surprisingly inside there was a lot of brass, and it had a good mixed clientele. It was packed and barely any place to sit, but two people were leaving, so we went over to grab their seats. We talked some more, and he gave me more advice and tips. It was interesting, but as we kept drinking, I wasn't getting tired and bored like I usually do. After about three beers, I usually get annoyed and start talking myself down and get real negative, and then I just don't want to talk to anyone. I get real self-critical. I stay stupid shit like, who the fuck would want me? I don't make enough money. I don't have that chiseled Brad Pitt look. I'm not famous. I'm just some dumb fuck sitting by himself in a bar looking like a pathetic loser. Women could probably smell my low self-esteem before entering the bar.

I felt alive tonight. I felt like I could do anything. The world seemed brighter and fuller of promise. There was no self-doubt. There was no dead end. If there were closed doors, I wanted to open them all. I wanted to be audacious and bold. I was carefree, thoughtless. My mind wasn't getting me down. My mind wasn't in my way. My mind was actually pushing me from behind, shoving me out the door. I had this compulsion, this rush, this need, this craving to make things happen, to talk to people, to dominate the conversation, to be the center of attention, to make people want me. It was unreal. I wish I had snorted this shit all my life.

He spotted a brunette at the end of the bar, sitting with these two guys, and there was an open seat. He told me to take it.

"What if they're all together?" I asked.

"I've been watching. They aren't. Go. Don't think, just go."

I walked over and immediately made eye contact. She looked away. I grabbed the seat. I ordered a beer and ignored her for a little. Back in the day, I'd just fucking sit there, seriously. I'd sit there talking to myself, making excuses, waiting for her to make the move, waiting for her to do something, just sit there and convince myself that it wasn't worth my effort, just make up excuses for not even trying. I fucking hated my old self. I used to be a loser.

Tonight I just turned around.

"What are you drinking?" I asked.

"Cosmo," she replied. "Like Sex and the City."

"Uh, what?"

"The TV show."

"Oh, there's a TV show called Sex and the City?"

"Yeah, it's on HBO."

"Oh, I don't have cable," shit I shouldn't have said that. Who doesn't have cable? Interestingly, in some weekly motels, they had cable.

"It's about these single, yuppie women who live in Manhattan. They're pretty cool, and they drink Cosmopolitan martinis."

"What's in it?"

"Vodka, Cointreau, lime juice, and cranberry juice. Would you like a taste?"

It tasted surprisingly good. I had tried a martini a long time ago and thought it tasted horrible. I hated olives.

"This is really good. It's funny, I tried a martini a while ago, and I thought it tasted awful. It was like a James Bond martini with an olive and gin. I'm not too fond of olives."

"Oh my, that sounds bad. Yes, martinis are back in style, but not the old school stuff."

"Shaken not stirred." She smiled. "I think I'll order myself one."

"So what brings you out tonight?" She turned towards me and started playing with her hair.

I never had such a beautiful woman be so receptive to me except Andrea. Maybe this one was a meth head too.

"Oh, I'm just hanging out with a friend of mine." I looked back, and Sean was talking to the cute waitress and making her smile and laugh.

"How do you guys know each other?"

"Oh, we actually work together." I wasn't about to tell her that Sean was my boss. I started to wonder if she was attracted to him like almost every woman in the universe.

"Oh, where do you work?"

"eGo."

"eGo?" she laughed.

"Yeah, I know it sounds weird. It's all about adding the letter 'e' to any word, and voila, you have a dot com company and you can go public and make lots of money."

"Hmmm, maybe I'll have to buy some shares."

"Hey, it's insider information, but I think we're doing pretty well."

She laughed. I couldn't believe how easy and smooth things were going, and she was smiling and laughing and playing with her hair.

"What brings you out tonight?" I asked.

"Oh, I'm actually here for the Safari Convention."

"The Safari Convention?"

"Oh yeah. It's this big game hunting convention."

"You hunt?"

"Oh no, honey. I do Marketing and Sales for charter jets. We charter flights for the hunters to Africa. They're from all over the world: Europe, New Zealand, Australia."

"Wow, that sounds fascinating," that sounded so cliché it was embarrassing. She smiled.

"How long are you in town?" I asked.

"I'm only here for a few more days."

"Have you been around town much?"

"Well, I'm staying at the Peppermill, but I've been around downtown. It's a small town."

"Well, yeah it's not exactly Vegas."

"The hunters actually like Reno, although I get the feeling, any time the convention could move to Vegas, but Reno is nice. It's more about nature, and it's more mellow and low key."

"Where are you from?"

"I'm actually from Vegas."

"Wow. I guess Reno must seem really small then."

"I like it. I have to visit the ladies room, I'll be right back."

I couldn't believe how well things were going. I looked over at Sean. He was now talking to a table full of women. They were all flirting with him. I tried to calm myself. I didn't want to screw this up. I remembered what Sean had told me: stop thinking, stop fucking thinking, stop fucking thinking. She returned.

"Look, I have to get back to the Peppermill, but tell you what, let me get your number, and maybe you can show me around this little town of yours tomorrow." I'm not sure whether at that point I was smiling like an idiot.

We met up tomorrow, and I drove her around and then we went to dinner, a bar, a strip club, and I dropped her off at the Peppermill. Just as she was getting out, she turned around and looked me in my eyes.

"You want to fuck me?"

After a few seconds of shock, I snapped out of it. "I'll go park the car."

I went up to her room and we went to her bed, and we had sex, but I was so drunk and tired, I honestly couldn't keep it up. I felt sort of embarrassed. I spent the night, but I couldn't really sleep. I didn't like sleeping in foreign environments, and I had to fart like crazy and I was worried that if I let one out in the bathroom it might be one of those loud hissy ones. The next morning, however, I went downstairs and farted my ass off in the casino restroom. I went back up and we then made out and fucked for an hour.

She said she had to go to the convention all day, so we met up that evening, and I took her back to my place, and we fucked that night and the next morning. I had never fucked so much in my life. I just couldn't get over why I never hit on more women before. This is what I was missing. What the fuck was wrong with me? I was living the dream. I'd wake up in the morning, check her body out, smile, tell myself, once she wakes up, I'll be fucking that ass! I was in the game. I was fucking a cheerleader!

On Monday, I went to Sean's office. I had told him about the whole weekend.

"So what do you get out of this?" I asked him. "What kind of bet is it where you only pay if you lose?"

"How about loyalty Bill? You don't ever cross me. You watch my back. If anyone out there is scheming against me, you let me know. You just got my back. And oh yeah, if you ever do write your great American novel, I want to be a character in it. You see the only way guys like me, men of action not words, get into novels is if some scrawny, nerdy type writes about us. No offense."

"No problem. Can I buy some coke off you?"

"Sure, an eight-ball is $150."

"What's an eight-ball?"

"Eighth of an ounce, 3.5 grams."

"Oh."

Looking back on the whole ordeal, it did occur to me that Sean might have just hired some escort and told her to meet us at Foley's that night. I'm not sure if he had intended on paying for a whole weekend with her. He might have been pissed off to find out that we fucked four times. What is that like a grand at least? I had her number, and I did go and visit her the following year in Vegas. We only fucked once. I didn't think she was a hooker, but my confidence was sky high now. Snorting a few lines and going out on the town, I was unstoppable. I was never as lucky as that night, though. In fact, as it turned out, I was hitting on a hundred women just to get a single one-night-stand. It could have been beginner's luck. She could have been a hooker. I did get one-night-stands though. I always kept in mind what Sean told me. Shoot lower. I wound up getting shorter, chubbier women, but I had more sex that year than all my life before that.

Chapter 9: Murder

The office was located right at the western edge of Reno near a large forest area, and in the summer time with very little precipitation, there were a lot of forest fires. One went right up to our warehouse. It was an exciting event. There was a real chance our warehouse and office would catch fire. Sam was useless. Sean jumped on the roof and hosed it down and kept watch for embers while smoke filled the whole place. He got IT to take all the servers home. Sam just kept going out and looking at the fire. The smell of that smoke was just amazing. My eyes burned. The fire department was evacuating everyone, but they let a few of us stay. It was almost as if those remaining wanted to show Sean that we would die for this stupid company and go down in flames with the ship. Near the end, it was only Sean, Sam, me, and Marla. Marla was still trying to kiss up to Sean and Sam. I'm pretty sure she had an affair with Sean that whore. They had been going out to lunch together recently, and I kept running into her in Sean's office. One time, I swear her hair was all messed up and it looked like they had just fucked. She wasn't all over Sam as usual. She knew who the alpha was. Sam was yesterday's news. Sam was becoming more and more irrelevant, secluded, and eccentric. Sure he was a millionaire now, but probably for the first time in his life, he didn't have any work to do. If I was him, I'd just check into the office an hour a day and then go out golfing or something. I was really tempted to ask Sean if he was hooking up with Marla, but somehow, I guess, I already knew the answer, but then again, it would have killed me to know it for sure.

Most everyone eventually left. They weren't as crazy or loyal I guess. I loved the danger, and I just kept working trying to pretend like nothing bothered me, like those dumb fucks who kept playing in the orchestra as the Titanic sunk. It was a total rush. Fortunately, the winds changed, and the whole place was saved. I finally gave in when I got tired and went home. I saw Sean and Sam's cars in the parking lot as I left. I had big pressure building up in my sinuses under my eyes from all the smoke.

That night, I was thinking about Marla a lot and suffered insomnia. On Monday, Marla didn't show up to work. She didn't call in sick. It was unlike her to no show. In fact, if anyone in the office was anal about showing up exactly on time, every single day, it was Marla. Sam asked me about her, but I told him I had no idea. Since it was so unusual of her not to show up, when lunch came around, Sam drove over to her house and then called her husband. The husband said he thought she went to work. She wasn't at home. It was the new gossip of the office. I suggested that we call all the local hospitals and someone even suggested calling the county jail. We made the calls, and she was in none of them.

I knew she had troubles with her husband, and he had been physical with her before. I also suspected that Sean was having an affair with her, but the stats always show that it is the husband first and then the boyfriend. But before I let my imagination get too loose, I figured she just slept over at some other guy's place and just slept in. By the end of the day, that scenario didn't work. Although, I thought you had to wait 24 hours to file a missing persons report, the police came in to talk with Sam. I wondered perhaps she may have gotten in a car accident, crashed in some ditch and was lying there hidden in a ditch. I decided after work to drive slowly from work back to her house.

That week, we created a missing person poster. One person suggested calling John Walsh and his show about missing people. She called the show but received no response. We posted the posters along the route Marla took from her home to work. We plastered her neighborhood with posters. Throughout all of this, her husband Tom didn't do a thing. He didn't seem the slightest bothered that she was missing, and we all started to suspect that he killed her. It was then that it finally started to sink in. Marla could be dead. Marla had told me a few days earlier that Tom made her cash out her shares of eGo, $50K worth. She was crying about it and told me that she didn't want to do it, but he said the stock was going to crash. I told her that he just wanted the money and told her never to give him any of it and divorce him.

Monday the office now was all abuzz with wild speculation about what could have happened. Maybe she decided she had had enough of life in Reno and just packed her bags and left town. But she had a daughter she loved. She would never ditch her without even saying a word. I started to obsess about the whole situation. Rumors started up that she had an argument with her husband over cashing out her eGo shares. Another rumor spread that her husband found out she was having an affair with Sean.

A police detective came by the office, and he interviewed the people who knew her best, and I was one of them. I told him that she was super reliable and loved her daughter, and it would be completely out of character for her to just pack her bags and go on a road trip. I told him about Tom making her cash out her eGo shares. I then told him about how close a relationship she had with Sam. I didn't feel like I was indicting Sam, but who knew, maybe Sam went off the deep end. I told him that Marla told me that she had been over to Sam's house, and they worked closely a lot before the company went public. I told him that after the company went public, Marla was not as involved in the company as much as before, but she still spent a lot of time with Sam. I told the detective that I had hung out with Marla a few times with the coworkers after work, but I didn't tell him that I went out with her alone, that we made out, that I lusted her and was deeply jealous that she was seeing Sean. I didn't mention Sean. I remembered what Sean had told me, watch his back. My loyalty was to Sean not Sam now. I didn't tell him that I suspected that Sean and Marla were fucking each other's brains out. I also realized that I could possibly be a suspect in this whole thing and wondered whether I should have gotten a lawyer before making my recorded statement to the detective.

There was just no way she was hiding from her husband without telling her daughter or Sam or Sean or anyone. There was no way she was on some weird road trip. She was probably dead, buried in her own backyard, maybe out in the desert somewhere, maybe down a mine shaft, who knew. On Wednesday, the local news interviewed us and we watched ourselves on the news. It was weird how it had now become a citywide event. It was weird how on the one hand it was a little bit of local celebrity, but on the other hand, it wasn't something you could cheer about or tell your friends. Then again, I didn't know anyone outside of work.

They called a counselor to the office, and we went in groups to talk with him. I had never been to therapy and had no idea what would happen. I imagined, he would just have us all talk about our feelings and sorrow. He went around the room and asked us what we were feeling and how we were coping with it. When he started talking to one of my workers, she started to cry. He continued probing her feelings, and it only seemed to make her cry even more. I was becoming disturbed. I thought he was going too far, and I told her she didn't have to keep answering his questions. I told her she didn't have to do this and could leave at any time. The counselor later talked to me one-on-one and told me that it was good for people to get it all out of their system, and he wasn't trying to hurt or humiliate her. I realized what an idiot I was. He told me that he appreciated how protective I was of her, and perhaps that too was one way I was dealing with this whole situation. I realized that I had no power to save Marla, but I guess I was being overly protective of everyone else. How could I have helped Marla? I told her to leave Tom. She stopped going out with me and had an affair with Sam and Sean. She blew me off. What could I have done? It was her choice.

By the end of the week, despair set in. The office took on a different feel, a different vibe. No one was kidding around or joking. It was quiet. Every now and then a female employee would start crying. I started avoiding the office, but then I realized that I didn't like staying at home either or day drinking at a bar, so I went back to the office. I realized that I actually needed all my coworkers for support. It just didn't seem to bother me that much, but maybe I was just sublimating my feelings. I just knew that I didn't want to be alone, and I needed to keep myself busy.

The third week, the police arrested her husband on check fraud charges. He had attempted to withdraw the $50K she got from selling her eGo shares from her checking account using a forged check. They never found the body for a murder trial. I saw her husband for the first time on

TV. He was nothing like I imagined for such a hot chick. He didn't even look like such a bad guy, but I guess that's what people thought about Ted Bundy.

A few weeks later, I was subpoenaed to testify for the prosecutors. I had never been called up for jury duty in Reno, and I always wanted to. Everyone says they try to avoid it, but I would love to sit in on a jury and even be sequestered for a week in a hotel and order room service and read books and watch TV all day.

Sean called me up to his office.

"So, you ever testified before?" he asked.

"No."

"Ever been questioned or interrogated by a detective or DA?"

"Nope."

He leaned toward me.

"Ever had someone trying to fuck with your mind? Get inside your head? Made you squirm?"

"Um, sometimes I guess. I guess, like a used car salesman or something."

"Yeah, that's a good example. Okay, young Jedi, Luke Skywalker, I'm going to give you a lesson my dad gave me. My dad was all about life lessons. He should have written a fucking book about it or something or started some motivational speaker thing. He was pretty good at it."

"My dad never even talked to me, my natural dad. It was like he thought his kids were pets. He'd pet us on the head after coming home from work and then just ignore us. Never took me out to throw a ball. No life lessons. No advice, nothing."

"Well Bill, that's the difference between the upper and lower classes. The lower classes are victims. They go through life eternally unprepared and like animals can only react to circumstances about only 15 minutes into the future, and that's all they see and plan for. Why teach a kid to plan further out? Why give the kid any life skills? All that shit just makes him over-think shit, and by the time he formulates a plan of action in that 15 minute window, it's all over and all his other poor competitors have already taken everything they need. In the upper classes, we don't let TV raise our children. That's like putting a dog in front of a nature channel and expecting the dog to grow up to be a perfectly obedient house pet. But you got me Bill. Don't think of me as your surrogate dad, god forbid –"

"Oh no, uh, if anything maybe a big brother."

"Yeah sure, whatever. A mentor. I'm going to give you a secret to leadership that will make 99% of the population follow you, do you favors, do your job, serve you, protect you. You want to own that court room Bill. You want to own the jury, the judge, and most importantly, you want to own the douchebag's defense lawyer. If they cross-examine you, they'll try to make you their bitch, and if they get under your skin, they'll be like your puppet master and do and say all sorts of shit that you don't want to."

"Okay, so how do I handle it?"

"Let me tell you a story my dad told me first. There's an old joke about an English ship Captain on the radio with an Irishman, and the English Captain discovers that they are on a collision course, so he demands that the Irishman change course as the English Captain knows his battleship is the largest ship on the sea, well at least he knows the Irish don't have battleships larger than the British. The Irishman demands that he changes course, but the English Captain is emphatic wondering if the Irish even have battleships. Finally, the English Captain demands to know what kind of ship the Irishman has and the Irishman replies, a lighthouse."

I cracked up.

"Of course, you know what I'm talking about. I'm not talking about sidestepping a fat dude on the sidewalk. I'm talking about smaller people, people with less character, will, determination, drive, power, authority, they move to the side when someone stronger comes along. And I'm not talking about sidewalks either; I'm talking about your disposition and demeanor. A fat, ugly dude walks into the party, you barely notice him. Your disposition and demeanor don't change. If he walks up to a group of you talking, and he's all cheery and enthused, you stop cracking jokes, you stop smiling, you start acting all stoic and reserved. He looks like a fool, so eventually he gets it and stops smiling, stops acting all dumb and cheery. Bam! They got him. Now, they all start cracking jokes, but it's not jokes in general, they're joking about him now. He doesn't have a clue. He starts smiling again. What an idiot.

Now, a beautiful, tall, confident woman walks into the party. Everyone notices her. She acts like she just walked into an empty room. Nobody in the room is worth her acknowledgement. She walks up to a group, and she's stoic, reserved, the buffoons in the group do their best to cheer her up, some idiots even try the old, 'hey, why the long face.' She ignores them all. Finally, the group settles down, and they become stoic and reserved. She smiles at them all, tells them to have a good evening, and trots off knowing they're all schmucks. You get it?"

"Yeah, just pick a demeanor and go with it no matter what."

"Right. Two more examples. You walk up to a group of kids in the street, and they're all like, 'Yo fuck you man, you're in the wrong neighborhood, get the fuck out asshole!' Now, your heart is all thumping and your hands are shaking, and your mouth is getting all dry. These kids own you. But what if you wanted to own them? Walk right up to them with a big shit-eating grin and go, 'Hey boys, what's happening? Looking for a gas station around here. One of you take me there, I'll buy you a candy bar.' They're all, 'fuck you asshole, get the fuck out of here.' And you're like, 'What, Snickers is too good for you? Who the fuck don't want a Snicker's bar? Don't listen to him,' point out the leader, 'I know you want a Snicker's bar!' They'll be all cracking up and shit and think you're cool. You own them. Two of them will help you find a gas station, then you buy one Snickers bar, and make them fight for it.

Second example, you walk up to two chicks and they're all smiling and joking with each other. You walk up and suddenly they stop talking, stop smiling. Meanwhile, you got a big smile, and you're trying to make friends. They're testing you. If they can get you to drop your smile, you're a pussy, they own you. So what do you do? Keep fucking smiling.

Pretend they're dressed in clown suits. Imagine them juggling kittens. Just act like you're all mad with a crazed grin. Crack a joke. Make them laugh. You make them smile and laugh you win, you own them. That's why it's easier to approach women being serious and stoic. It's a game, who can change whose demeanor first."

"You know, that's my biggest problem. If I walk up to a woman, and I'm trying to be friendly and she's all acting bitchy, upset, reserved, apathetic, that really pisses me off. I get all mad."

"No, you're taking her lead doofus. You're letting her control you like you're her bitch. You're like, hey, if a chick smiles and laughs with me, why that makes me so happy and joyful, and when a chick is serious and uninterested, why that makes me so mad and crazy. You're letting them control you and not vice versa. When a chick plays opposite demeanors with you, she's testing you, seeing if you're a follower or a leader. Look, you ever get caught in the serendipity trap?"

"No, what do you mean?"

"Okay, you're walking down the street and all the sudden you have a craving for fried chicken, KFC fried chicken. Then low and behold, you see an ad on a passing bus for KFC, and then low and behold, you see a KFC across the street. So you cross the street but get hit by a bus and die. You get it? You're a rebel. You think you're following your instincts and urges, thinking, as long as I'm following my instincts and my urges, I'm free, I'm my own person. But no, you don't get it. Unless you live alone in a cave, everyone and everything is depositing little seeds of urges in you, and when they sprout, you think they belong to you when in fact; they belong to whoever deposited it in your mind. No shit, you crave KFC out of the blue, because the last week KFC has been bombarding TV with ads. Get it? They been putting ads on buses, bus shelters, billboards, newspapers, and all this time, you think you're the one who came up with the urge. That's how manipulators work. They sow seeds into your brain, and when they sprout, you think you put them there. A car salesman will tell you how cool a big engine is and then question you about whether a small car is safe. A few minutes later, you suddenly get an urge for a big engine in a big car, and you thought it was your idea. Walk up to a woman and just say the word 'date' like, I just had a salad with dates, and then go back and a few minutes later ask her for a date, and she'll think it's serendipity. It's the serendipity trap. Don't fall for it. That's why you don't always follow your urges and instincts, because a lot of times, they're not yours."

"Okay, so how does this all help me testify?"

"Okay, so walk into the courtroom and don't look at anyone. Just look straight ahead like you're walking into an empty room. Then after taking the stand, make eye contact with the defense attorney first then the jury, each and every one, then the judge, and smile. And don't ever stop smiling. Whatever the first questions, load your answers with positive words: honest, reliable, truth, helpful, good, kind, dependable. *Bill Keane, how long have you known Marla?* 'A good year and a half.' *How would you describe your relationship with her?* 'We were good coworkers, and she was very reliable and dependable. To be honest, I felt I could really trust her, and she always appreciated how helpful I was to her, especially through the hard times she had with her abusive husband.' "

"Wow."

"Get it? Seeds of trust. Seeds of doubt. Then just sit back, smile, let them sprout. No matter how pissy, angry, annoying, rude the defense attorney gets with you, take a breath, smile, and stay cheerful. If you start panicking and lose your charm, confidence, and cheerfulness, the defense attorney will eat you, the judge will ignore pleas from the prosecutor, and the jury will laugh at you squirm. Own that courtroom, fact, own everything in life Bill. Quit being that badass dichotomy rebel and following what you think are your instincts and urges. Get disciplined. Create your own long-term plan and keep to it. Lead yourself, and you'll lead others. And lastly, don't fucking mention that I fucked Marla, that was all Sam. Marla was like a fucking sister to me."

I went to a casino and had a beer before walking over to the courthouse. I had never been inside a courtroom except in a stupid small claims thing and a speeding ticket. I had never dealt with a full jury. I was first placed in the DA's office, and there were relatives of Marla there crying. I didn't approach them. I didn't know them, and I didn't want to introduce myself.

They then took me to just outside the courtroom. There were benches along the wall, and I sat there, stood up, sat, stood up. I was restless and nervous. They called me in. I walked down the aisle and noticed Tom sitting on the left. He didn't acknowledge me. I thought it was just so bizarre how I was walking so close to a fucking murderer. I went to the witness box keeping in mind what Sean had told me. It was just like what I had seen in any courtroom drama. I looked at the defense attorney, looked over at the jury, then looked at the judge, then smiled like I just farted exiting my friend's car.

The prosecutors asked me some general questions, my name, my occupation, how long I had worked with Marla, when she went missing, etc. It was brief and easy. The defense didn't cross examine me.

They found Tom guilty of check fraud and sentenced him to ten years. I considered killing the fuck when they released him.

Chapter 10: Gluttony and Sloth

Meanwhile eGo went up to $40 a share. If Marla's husband had just waited a couple more months, he could have made a shitload more money. Maybe she took him out of her will. Sean was spending more money than he knew what to do with it. He gave me another generous raise and put me in charge of the data entry department. He then sent me out on trips to New York for workshops and training classes. You'd be amazed at how many bullshit classes are out there to improve your career skills.

My first trip to New York I flew business class. I had never flown business class in my life. It was so much nicer with more leg space, wider seats, and the flight attendants were younger and hotter. I guess back in the day, when flying was new, it was pretty much reserved for the upper class. This attracted a lot of young, hot stewardesses who were basically hot cocktail waitresses. But then as they expanded to the middle class, the young stewardesses became 30-something flight attendants. Then came the budget and discount airlines, and now the 30-something's were 40 and 50-something's.

I was now living the life. Styling. Flying business class on a business trip. I couldn't believe it. I couldn't stop smiling. I felt important, special, for the first time in my life. The first thing I noticed when I stepped off the plane at JFK onto the jet way was the humidity. Reno is like one of the driest places in America. It hardly ever rains, and the air is also thin from high altitude. It got humid in San Francisco, but New York was unreal. You could feel the air roll over your body.

When I was in the airport I just couldn't believe I was in New York City. Walking through the airport, I started to notice that almost every clerk at all the stores and restaurants were black or Latino. I had been living in Reno too long. Reno service workers were almost all white.

When I traveled, I usually took a shuttle van from the airport to the hotel, but Sean told me to take a cab and charge it to my credit card he set up for me. He taught me how to do expense vouchers, but he also taught me how to inflate my expenses, charge all sorts of shit to the card including meals and clothes. He told me where I could go charge a $3000 suit to my card, photocopy the receipt as a business expense, go back to the store, return the suit and get cash back. When I went there, some Australian dude told me to order a suit, pay up front, he'd tell me the suit I wanted was not available, and he would give me a cash refund on the spot, but they took a 20% "restocking fee" for a suit they didn't even have. So I walked out with $2400, and he made $600 for a minute of work. What a fucking scam. "Good on ya mate," he'd keep saying and, "cheers." Every time I go to Outback now, I can't help but remember him. The dude there also hooked me up with a coke dealer, but it wasn't $150 an eight-ball like in Reno, it was $150 a gram, and it was literally three-and-a-half times as good. The first time I did it, I was literally crawling up the walls of my hotel, sucking on my dry mouth, drinking about a gallon of bathroom faucet water, jogging in place. I thought they accidentally gave me meth. I was tweaking like a meth head. I almost called Sean, telling him to talk me down and shit, but fortunately I didn't. I quickly adjusted my doses. Three and half lines of Reno shit was the same as one line of New York shit.

My hotel room was unbelievable. I had usually stayed in Motel 6 wherever I traveled. Those white plastic cups they wrap in transparent plastic wrap, the sink outside the bathroom with the closet with no doors, the manual AC/heater, the light they always leave on for you, the orange plastic diamond room number placard attached to the key. I was staying at the Grand Hyatt on 42nd Street. The lobby was amazing. There was marble everywhere. How could I even belong here? A few months ago I was living in a fucking weekly motel built in the 1950's with what looked like blood stains on the headboard perhaps from some unlucky fuck who blew his brains out from losing all his money gambling. How the hell did I end up at the Grand Hyatt in Manhattan? How? I looked around and noticed that I was the only idiot with a military duffle bag and a rolling duffle bag, and that week, I went out to a luggage store and upgraded to a Samsonite rolling hard case. I'll never forget the nice lining inside the case. It was unreal. I charged it to my travel expenses, $300. I bought a garment bag for my suits too. I made fake charges for suits for cash, but I actually wound up buying a $500 suit and several $200 sport coats at Macy's on other trips to New York. I charged them all to my travel expenses. I can just imagine some auditor wondering, why is this guy buying $3000 suits one day and $200 sport coats the other?

Sean told me my daily meal limit was $200. There was an Irish bar and restaurant on 2nd Avenue that would put most all my drink orders under food. I was a regular at that bar, and I could easily rack up $100 dollars in food and $100 in drinks, but the bill would be all $200 for food. One night, I gave out my very first $100 tip to some Irish chick from Ireland. I asked her out the next night and got rejected. I wish I didn't tip her $100. What the fuck right? I finally asked her, "Okay, so what's the likelihood of you ever going out with me? Maybe or no chance in hell?" I don't know why I asked her that question. She replied, "No chance in hell." I was so humiliated.

My hotel room was amazing. The view was amazing. I had one of those *Pretty Woman* moments when I felt like jumping up and down on the bed. I was giddy as a school girl on her first day of elementary school. For whatever reason, it wasn't the room that impressed me nearly as much as the bathroom. The bathroom was amazing. The tray full of free shit was amazing. Every time I went to New York, I'd take all the shampoo each day, and the maid would give me a new one each day. I later learned to leave a $2 tip every day on the nightstand. Sean told me once that it's good insurance that they don't scrub the toilet with your toothbrush. I wondered how many times they had done that my first trip to New York.

One day, I was so fucking stupid, I left my $2400 suit cash on the desk, and the hotel manager called me and told me not to do it and there was a safe in the closet. I was so embarrassed. I had so much money I swear I was probably dropping it on the street and in bars and leaving it in cabs. There were nights I had no idea how I could possibly blow through $200 in cash. I never imagined the day I would be taking out $200 a day from an ATM. I started to notice that some bartenders would short change me, so I devised a system to protect myself. I got a wallet with a divide in the cash area. I'd put my small bills in one area and my twenties in the other. That way, I wouldn't accidentally hand someone a twenty stuck between two tens thinking it was a ten. Second, I divided my twenties into $100 sets, and I'd use one twenty to wrap that set up. So I knew every time I was breaking open a new $100 set. Third, at the beginning of the night, I broke up all my twenties, so by the end of the night, I was just handing over fives and tens and getting small change back.

My first night out, Mike met up with me. He was Sean's friend and worked in the same bank that underwrote eGo. He pulled up to the valet in a Jaguar X308 (with a 4.0 Liter V8 engine that roared). This baby roared like Sean's Beemer.

"Bill?" Mike was half Puerto Rican, half Polish. He had tan skin; a goatee; a nice, silk, shiny, dark blue suit; and black dress shoes that were almost as polished as military dress shoes.

"Yeah, Mike?"

"Yo, what the deelio?"

What the what, I was thinking to myself.

"Welcome to New Yalk, first time?" He gave me this odd New York greeting where you cross your thumbs and wrap your fingers around the back of the other guy's hand, bring him towards your chest, and then pat the guy's back with your free hand. I must have looked stupid doing it for the first time.

"Yeah, first time."

"Mike will take care of you. Mike will show you the town." I thought he was Mike. At first, I was going, okay, your friend's name is Mike too? When we going to meet him? Then I soon realized he was talking about himself in the third person.

We jumped in his Jaguar. The interior was all leather and glassy wood. It was also pretty low to the floor. I had never been in a car so low to the ground. You could almost look up women's skirts. It wasn't as spacious as I had imagined, nothing like my Buick Regal or Mercury Grand Marquis, but then again, who gives a fuck right?

"So you're from Reno. Reno, where the fuck is that? Next to Vegas?"

"Um, no, Vegas is like 400 miles south of us."

"No shit! Nevada must be huge. You go 400 miles south of New York City you cross four states. Yeah Sean told me he lived in Reno now, some hick town with trailer parks. No offense."

"No offense taken. I originally grew up near Seattle and lived in San Francisco. I've only been in Reno a couple years. You've heard of the Mustang Ranch?"

"Oh yeah, the brothel. That's right, prostitution is legal in Nevada."

"We're close to Mustang Ranch."

"Nice. You been there?"

"No, not yet," I smiled.

Mike looked over at me. "We got them here in New York too, but they're called escorts. Yeah, that's the classy name for whores. Mike will take care of you," he smiled. "A-ight! We're going to China Club now."

"What is that, some club where you meet Chinese women?"

"Basically," he laughed. "No man, it's the hottest club in New York. It's where all the celebrities hang out."

"Nice."

"Better yet, it's where all the hot models go to pick up on the celebrities, but they don't know Mike's better than a celebrity. It's all about your machismo. They don't know Mike, and Mike's got machismo!"

At the club, I was so full of excitement and awe and wonder, I tried all these crazy cocktails with vodka, whisky, rum, tequila. The night was a blur. There was an outside area upstairs in the club. I was in la-la-land. The women were like models, in fact, I think many were. They were all dressed up in these beautiful long dresses with spaghetti straps. You would never see shit like that in Reno. They were all so tall, especially in high heels. I saw more hot women at that club than all my time in Reno, or even San Francisco for that matter. I guess there were hotties in San

Francisco, but I never went to fancy clubs or restaurants. I was definitely out of my league, but I was so drunk I didn't care. They had no idea I was some kid from Reno who just recently lived in a weekly motel. As far as they were concerned, I could be a millionaire Wall Street financier, although, in hindsight, I was still at Macy's level fashion. These guys were like Nieman Marcus and later on, I discovered people like these, they shop at the designer's own stores. I didn't even know there were different levels of Armani: Armani Privé at the top, Giorgio Armani, Emporio Armani, Armani Collezioni, Armani Exchange, then the Chinese knock-off's Armoni and Armanzi.

At the end of the night, I could barely walk. Mike had to walk me to his car, drive slowly so I didn't throw up on his nice leather, and walk me all the way to my hotel door. It was weird, but I had just met Mike a few hours ago, and I felt like my life was in his hands, and he was looking after me like a big brother. Maybe that's how you bond with guys, just go out and get trashed and you put yourself in their hands. I passed out and then in the middle of the night threw up on the carpet. I thought about trying to clean it up the next morning, but I decided, isn't that what maids do? Mike later told me I should have tipped the maid a hundred bucks. I felt bad about that later. In hindsight, I'm pretty sure the maid must have scrubbed the toilet with my toothbrush.

The next morning, I was sick as hell. I took a cab to the workshop on risk management so ironically. I was late. Other than that morning, I never skipped a minute of the workshop, but after a few workshops later, I realized that a lot of people just showed up the first day and last day to get the certificate. After a while, I was the doing exact same thing, partying every night of the week, and then showing up the last day to take the certificate. The teachers didn't give a shit. They knew the scam too. They were getting paid for 40 students whether 10 or 20 showed up or 40. I'd only go to class if the teacher was hot, stay after, ask her out, get shot down, then never come back until the last day.

But I behaved that first week. I don't know what it was about that first week, the humidity, the senses, the atmosphere, the novelty, the shock. It was like a dream. Every once in a while, when I return to New York or any city with a lot of humidity, I get that sensation again, that rhythm, that vibe, that sensation, that wonder, that dreamy feel of that first week. It was the best week of my life up to that point. It was the apex of my life. I was on top of the world. I had more money than I knew what to do with it, I had my youth, I had new confidence and skills, I didn't have to work that hard, it was as close to heaven as I could possibly imagine heaven to be. In hindsight, I have to wonder whether it's better to expose a young 20-something to such dizzying heights of luxury, because there's no other way but to go down. Is it better to have been on top so young and crash or never to have been on top? Of course, I'd never take it back. Of course, it's better to just get progressively better and better things in life, but then again, hell, who gives a fuck if you're 60 and driving a $100K car. Ironically, those $100K cars, those hot models, they're better spent on 20-somethings who need them more and appreciate them more than 60 year-old fucks popping Viagra.

In the evenings, Mike showed me a whole world I never knew existed. I had seen New York from watching "Seinfeld" and "Friends," but that was like experiencing Tokyo by watching a Godzilla movie. The streets of Manhattan were just unreal. San Francisco streets were crowded and busy, but Manhattan was ten times that, and unlike San Francisco, they didn't stink of urine, and you didn't get assaulted by panhandlers every block. Rudy Giuliani and Bill Bratton, the police chief really had cleaned up New York. When I grew up, I always heard stories of crime in New York City. I watched *The Warriors* and *Escape from New York*. Back then, they told you never to make eye contact with anyone on the streets. I was ready to confront gangs and thugs in New York City, but after a while, I wasn't even looking over my shoulder walking down the streets drunk at 2 AM.

The New York I experienced was like Disneyland. People were happy, friendly, outgoing, charismatic, loud, carefree. There were thugs around, but it all depended on what part of town you were in: uptown, Harlem, midtown, Times Square, 30's, downtown. I particularly liked downtown with the somewhat slower pace, smaller buildings, small neighborhood feel, especially around NYU. Mike called me gay for hanging out downtown, and called it, "a cesspool of bohemian wannabe artists, queers, and weird ethnic folk with their stinking food." He was half Puerto Rican, but I think he was kidding.

"They should put up like a 100-foot wall around downtown New York, like that movie *Escape from New York* but just downtown," he went on. "That way you keep their stinking garlic from drifting uptown. You'd have to carve out a corridor for Wall Street. It don't matter what race they are, Italian, Korean, them ethnic fuckers all cook with too much garlic." I wasn't quite sure if he was kidding or not.

Mike introduced me to New York culture. He kept referring to himself in the third person and then just out of the blue would come up with the most obscene, graphic remarks, "Mike does very well with the ladies. Mike will shove his cock down that chick's throat and spray cum all over her bedroom walls like a lawn sprinkler!" He would make that sputtering noise like a lawn sprinkler. "I'll make her scream three times, first when I fuck her pussy real hard, then when I cum on her face, then when I wipe my dick off with her silk sheets." We'd be standing in line at a deli, at a bar, in a coffee shop, just out of the blue, graphic, explicit, raw, obscene non sequitur sexual comments. There would be more than one time some woman behind us or next to us would look over in shock. "Look at her, I bet she was screaming hot say ten, fifteen years ago. Those big tits. I'd just fuck those tits, put my dick between them and go to town. You ever done that? But I'd do it facing her feet so she could lick my asshole." Are you fucking kidding me? He said that as we sat next to table full of tourists, a couple with their three daughters. "Ugly chicks need loving too, and that's why God created assholes for them to lick." Jesus.

He was fucking hilarious and crazy. He'd also get smashed and black out and get into fights. He was a bad ass. He wouldn't even give a dude the chance to back down. After a while, I could read him telegraphing his punch. He'd look away, lower his left shoulder, drop his left hand, then in one sudden explosive twitch land an uppercut right to some poor dude's face often knocking him to the floor. Only once did he get his ass kicked, and I had to jump in and pull some dude off him. Mike was also big into coke, and you could tell when he just did a few lines, he'd come back all wired, fingers twitching, eyes bouncing all over, sniffling like he had a cold, and then invariably he'd get Tourette's and start shoving guys and getting into fights. "Fuck, dick, cunt, shit ass, bitch, whore, mother fucking, twat, fuck, shit ass, monkey fucking, ass licking, puke face loser bitch pig cunt, I wouldn't fuck her with Al Roker's fat black dick."

Like me, he had a fucked up mother who often abused him, he confessed one night in a drunken stupor, except his mother used to physically abuse him whereas my mother's abuse was emotional, verbal, and psychological. You never hear about abusive mothers, but we were a pair of them, and it was interesting to see how it manifested in our subtle misogynistic jokes as well as over-the-top rants.

He kept saying, "basically" whenever I made some observational remark.

"There's like a pizza and deli on almost every block," I'd say.

"Basically," he'd reply.

He would also keep saying, "A-ight!" and, "nigga pleeeeeeeease" of course, back in the day when everyone was throwing around that term. He did a gay Puerto Rican impression that is probably way too offensive to portray anywhere outside of a group of exclusively gay Puerto Ricans. "Oh papi, shove that fat hot chorizo up my culo. Uh-oh, oh no you de'nt, it went all limp chico malo." He cracked me up constantly. There were many times I was bowled over laughing, stomach aching, tears streaming down my eyes. I had never been around someone so full of life and on fire. Maybe it was the coke, but he was like barreling 100 MPH through life in addition to literally in his Jaguar. I often wondered how he never got a DUI. One night I threw up on the side of his car, and he wasn't too happy about that the next morning. You don't get a paint job for $200 at Earl Scheib for a brand new Jaguar X308. It would cost like $10K. He said the acid in my stomach could erode the paint. I felt pretty bad, but fuck if I was paying him $10K.

Sometimes he'd ask me, "You a'ight?"

I'd be thinking to myself, is there something that looks wrong with me? Do I look angry? Tired? Upset? Then I finally got it. It was a fucking greeting, like, "How you doin?" You don't reply, "Oh, I'm okay, but I have a little sore back." They don't give a fuck how you're doing. It's a greeting.

He introduced me to knishes which I loved. I put ketchup on it first, but when he told me you eat it with mustard, it was just mind blowing. He had a Jewish friend, Jim who introduced me to gefilte fish, vareniki, matzah balls, reuben sandwiches, latkas, rugelach, kasha varnishkas, chocolate babka's, challah rolls, Pirozhki's, bagel and lox, and goulash. I loved Pirozhki's and vareniki's. I couldn't believe I had not opened my mind up to all the possibilities of the world. I lived in fucking Reno. I may have experienced culture and cuisine in San Francisco, but New York City was like a different planet. Every time I went back to Reno, I'd go to Tony's pizza and Newman's deli, somehow in that food connection, somehow jump right back into Manhattan.

I also started to notice that there were a lot of Jews in Manhattan, and I started to pick up on the Jewish culture, or at least the Jewish-American culture. "Oye veh!" I told Jim I learned a lot about New York from the TV shows "Friends" and "Seinfeld" but he told me "Friends" and "Seinfeld" were filmed in California, and the street scenes made New York look like Disneyland.

"And those apartments they live in," he continued. "Don't get me started. They like work in a coffee shop and Joey's an aspiring actor, and that two-bedroom apartment must be like $2000. But I'll tell you what's authentic about "Seinfeld", they're all Jewish."

"What?"

"Yeah, you didn't know that? They're all Jews."

"I didn't know that."

"You ever heard that Chanukah song by Adam Sandler?"

"Oh yeah, like William Shatner and Leonard Nemoy are Jewish."

"Yeah, everyone in TV is Jewish. But it's not like a conspiracy, don't get me wrong. You see, back in the day, there was, well, you heard of the glass ceiling for women right?"

"Yeah."

"Well, there was a WASP ceiling back in the day. It wasn't just Jews, but Catholics, Poles, Irish, Italians. That's why the Italians had the mob, the Irish became police officers, and the Jews went into TV and film. The WASP's had all the good jobs, jobs with security and lots of money. You see all the famous Jews right, but you don't see the tens of thousands of Jews working as waiters trying to make it big. In fact, back in the day, many Jews were great athletes like the blacks today. It's not because we had any better genes, it's just one of those professions where 99% make nothing and 1% make it big time. Why do you think Mexicans are such great boxers? Same deal. You know bars and restaurants are the worst business investments? Like 80% of them fail in the first year. So who has all the bars? The Irish. Who has all the restaurants? The Italians, Chinese, the Jewish deli's. That's also the way it is with acting, writing, directing, producing. Except that failure rate is probably around 99.99%. For every one movie you see in a movie theater, there's probably a thousand that were made and lost money you never see. You have any idea how many producers lose money on movies? It's this big money-losing charity to artists. It's like Who's Who books. Nobody buys them but the people in them. You have to be an idiot to produce a movie, so WASP's, they don't invest in movies, they invest in stocks and real estate. People think the Jews own Hollywood and media, but you know what, we've paid the price. Countless Jews, hundreds of thousands have gone bankrupt in Hollywood pursuing their dreams. So 0.01% make it big time, and all the sudden, there's a conspiracy of Jews."

I honestly had thought there was this media cabal of Jews, but Jim changed my entire view of things. It's funny, but if you don't know any Jews, you see them as this one big group, this foreign entity that may be threatening, but hanging around Jim, I really started to fall in love with Jewish culture. I definitely identified with the oppressed race, the outcast identity. I could not imagine if my ancestors had been rounded up by the millions and murdered. It would definitely, fundamentally alter my view of the world and its treatment of my people and my identity, to live in a world so hostile to my people, a world that would kill six million of my people, and now a world that thinks my people own Hollywood and have some sort of secret plot to rule the world.

Jim tried to set me up with Jewish women. "You need a nice Jewish woman my friend. You're gentile, but don't worry, the Jewish line goes through the woman, so you're not taking away her heritage or the children. You raise them Jewish, you give them a bar mitzvah, everything works out."

I had to admit, I didn't even know what a Jewish woman looked like. I imagined they must all look like Elaine on "Seinfeld", but there were really all sorts, not just the dark, curly haired. There were some very exotic ones with the most amazing eyes, redheads, blondes, tall, short, skinny, fat, some were rowdy, loud, cussed like sailors, others were painfully shy, awkward, quiet. I started seriously considering hooking up with a Jewish woman, but it seemed, our dates never really went anywhere, and once they found out I lived out west, they didn't really take me seriously. It was just so odd how in New York City of all places, there were so many people still tied closely to their roots. There were Italian-American chicks I really dug that wouldn't even give me the time of day, because I wasn't Italian or probably worse, I wasn't Catholic. I even tried hooking up with this one amazingly beautiful Ethiopian Jewish woman, but she told me her family would never approve. What is this like 580 AD?

He also took me to a synagogue and showed me Hasidic Jews with their funny hair and hats.

In addition to Jewish food, I had an incredible food adventure in New York. I had White Castle burgers, Tastykake's which were so much better than Hostess, Yuengling beer, Neuhaus truffles, Junior's cheesecake, Oysters Rockefeller, a Waldorf Salad, and all sorts of steaks: porterhouse, steak Diane, rib eye, T-bone, prime rib, chateaubriand. I had prime rib in Reno, but it was like a half-inch thick and dry and $9.99. The prime rib in New York was two inches, succulent, and $30. I learned that prime rib was the same cut as rib eye, just roasted whole first.

I had all sorts of seafood. Reno has all-you-can-eat sushi, an embarrassment and insult to Japanese culture, like what Taco Bell does to

Mexican food. And most Reno folk will only eat salmon or tuna. Sushi in New York City was ala carte and the real deal, served by Japanese chefs not Mexican or Polynesian chefs like in Reno. I had Chilean Sea Bass that melted in my mouth, king crab legs of a mindboggling size, huge lobster that was killed that night for you, scallops the size of Reno filet mignon, mussels, oysters, crab cakes that would make your stomach cum, and one night near Christopher Street, we had paella that was ultra-orgasmic like coming on coke. And I thought Popeye's jambalaya was good.

Every time I went to New York, it would be a whirlwind culinary adventure: Spanish tapas, Korean BBQ grilled at your table, Ethiopian food with Injera bread and no utensils, Mediterranean food sitting on pillows with belly dancers, real Chinese food with screaming chefs and not a white person in sight, Polish food with hot waitresses from Poland, Cuban sandwiches, Turkish, Indonesian, and Malaysian.

I fell in love with New York, but I knew without my job at eGo, I had no way of living in such an expensive city. I could certainly live there and get some data entry job and share a cockroach, rat-infested closet-sized apartment in the 30's, but that wouldn't be the same as living at the Grand Hyatt with a $200 a day drinking and eating tab. I even checked out some apartments downtown and came to the quick, unpleasant realization that I was just kidding myself. Visit New York as a king or live in New York as a peasant. I'll never forget the 70's gold-laced mirror in this one shithole apartment off Christopher Street. How could I go from the Grand Hyatt to a shithole? I realized I was living on borrowed time. At first, I didn't know when the party would all end, but after a while, I just didn't care. At first, I couldn't comprehend why anyone would go watch a movie in Manhattan when there was so much else to do, but after my sixth visit, one night with nothing to do, I went and saw a movie, *The 13th Warrior*. It wasn't a nonstop party. I once found myself walking up and down 2nd Avenue from 42nd Street down to 20th and back. I was on top of the world, but it also sort of nagged me that I didn't have a girlfriend to share it all with.

The best part, however, were the women. Not only was I getting one-night-stands with professional 30-something's at bars and clubs, telling them that I was basically Sean, sent to some shithole Podunk to run a startup IPO. When I couldn't get laid that route, I just hired $500 escorts: tall, leggy, busty, bombshell Russian and Czech women. Mike hooked me up with a reliable escort service. Mike took care of Bill. Sometimes I'd get an escort right after a date with some tease. I had no idea women this beautiful even existed. Some were cold and distant, some seemed high off their asses, but the best were the ones who just wanted to have fun and party and talk. They loved it when I would do lines off their tits, and they would do lines off my dick and then suck it off and go all numb and laugh. The first time I almost cut the lines on her tit with a razor. Shit, what was I thinking? She said, "You want me to cut up some lines with a razor on your dick?" I got so spoiled on them, when I returned to Reno I felt I was going from the Miss Universe beauty pageant to the Miss Rodeo beauty pageant.

One night after screwing this Russian real hard off coke and getting an insane orgasm, I was lying around wondering whether to pay her another $500 for another round. We just sat there on the bed, and I acted like she was my girlfriend. I put my arm around her, and we intertwined our fingers.

"So what is Russia like? Cold?"

"I don't want to talk about it."

"Why not?" I persisted ignorantly. As far as I was concerned, you should be able to talk about anything unless it incriminates you. This was before I learned a thing or two about personal boundaries. I once fantasized meeting some woman and telling her all my secrets, and she would tell me all her secrets, and we wouldn't have any more secrets, and we would be intertwined on such a higher level. What an idiot I was.

"You want to know about Russia? This isn't small talk. I can tell you, Russia's beautiful. Nice looking mountain ranges. Forests and rivers and all the fucking cute animals, Bambi and rabbits and shit."

"That sounds nice." I was a bit groggy. I was having second thoughts about going another round.

"Fucking Americans. You have no idea. Your media makes you think the whole world is a fucking cartoon. You have no connection to the outside world, but your government fucks with everyone, and you have no responsibility for your government."

"How do we fuck everyone? We liberated the world from the Nazi's and helped you get rid of Communism."

"Oh I'm so fucking grateful! We were better off with Communism."

I turned and looked at her with surprise. She was getting upset, but I kind of liked being with an angry, naked, hot babe in bed. It was odd, but it was kind of cool.

"How can you say that?"

"You have any fucking idea what is going on in Russia today Sean?" I told her my name was Sean. She told me her name was Caroline, but it was probably Karolina or maybe Ivana.

"I know the economy's not doing so well."

"Not doing so well? Fuck! That's what you Americans think. Not so good. Not so bad. We are in a Depression! Fucking Yeltsin, that fat drunk, he handed over all of Russia's capital to the oligarchs. And your western media turned a blind eye. That fucking idiot attacked the parliament, like your Congress. What would happen if Bill Clinton ordered tanks to fire on Congress? The western media, again, turned a blind eye. Hundreds of millions of Russians starving, unemployed, soldiers with no pay, homeless, mafia thugs go around killing anyone they want, former KGB working for the oligarchs as bodyguards. All the men are alcoholics and all the women are prostitutes. I am a graduate student. I had a Master's degree in Engineering. Fucking clients think I'm some ignorant, high school educated kid, like an American, a hooker on drugs who can't even get a job as a receptionist. That $500 you pay me for one hour, I make more in an hour than most Russians do in three months. This is why I'm a fucking hooker."

I held her tighter. I'm not quite sure what the gesture meant, maybe that I didn't view her as a hooker, a $500 piece of meat.

"I had no idea."

"Americans have no idea. They are just happy. Buying all this shit, making all this money, throwing it all away. Even your homeless people wear Nike's. You Americans are like happy idiots. But it will not last forever. That is reality. You think Germany in the 30's would suffer and nothing would happen. Russia will find its own Hitler, an autocrat who will bring back the KGB, take back the old Soviet republics, maybe start World War III. Then America will not be very happy. No more fucking Happy Meal for America." I almost laughed.

"We are a stupid bunch of idiots aren't we?" I stroked her hair and looked her in the eyes.

"You want to fuck me again?" she asked. She grabbed my semi-hard dick and started rubbing it. I started playing with her amazing, perky tits. She was so hot. I felt sorry for her country, for all the suffering, for her family, for her, but at that moment, I just wanted to fuck her brains out. Most all escorts don't like to kiss, but I loved trying to kiss them. I'd tip them an extra $100. I didn't care if they thought it was too intimate or anything. What the fuck is sexual intercourse, a handshake? I shoved my tongue in her mouth and shoved my dick in her. It was the best, guilty sex I ever had in my life. I never had a Russian escort again. I started asking for Czech ones.

Mike kept going to the China Club on 47th Street and 8th Avenue. It was pretty hard to get into, but Mike had connections. I'll never forget the night I met Woody Harrelson there. It was unreal. We talked briefly.

"Have you seen *The Hi-Lo Country*?"

"No," I replied.

"*The Thin Red Line*?"

"No."

"How about *Wag the Dog*? *Welcome to Sarajevo*?"

"No."

"Do you know who the fuck I am?"

"Yeah, of course, "Cheers" Woody."

"*People vs. Larry Flynt?*"

"No, but I saw trailers, got you an Oscar right?"

"No, I was fucking nominated."

"Oh sorry."

"Have you seen any of my fucking movies?"

"*Natural Born Killers.*"

"Fuck, finally. Yeah, that was a while ago. Did you like it?"

"Uh, it was weird. Lots of blood and stuff."

"Well fuck yeah, it's called *Natural Born Killers* not um, what's the flying nun?"

"Oh, uh, uh, *Mary Poppins*?"

"Yeah, *Mary Poppins*, it's not fucking *Mary* fucking *Poppins*."

"So I was just curious, I mean, everywhere you go people recognize you. You get tired of that shit? You just want to be anonymous sometime?"

"Um yeah, if I wanted to be fucking anonymous I would have picked a different line of work like say managing actors. What do you do if I may be so bold?"

"Oh, I'm a financial analyst."

"So you analyze like financial matters?"

"Pretty much, not as interesting as what you do."

"Look, hey man, the world needs financial analyzers. You doing just as much as I am man. Fuck, some people don't even watch my movies. I won't name names, but I'm just saying. Sometimes I'm out there giving the performance of a lifetime, and you know what, nobody goes and watches, so it's like what the fuck am I doing it for right? But I'm doing it for me, you know. If everyone disappeared, I'd be up there, on a stage somewhere, I'd be acting out every character in the play. It's like not being who you are, but being what you are, do you get me? Are you with me, uh, what's your name?"

"Bill."

"Bill, Bill. You go around life acting out this person Bill right. You think you know Bill, but Bill, you don't fucking know Bill. You know why? Bill?"

"No, why?"

"Because all your life, other people tell you who Bill is. It ain't you though. But you believe them, so all your life, you pretend to be this Bill, and it ain't you. But you act man, try acting man, and even though you're pretending to be some fictitious thing, this other person that doesn't exist but is some figment of someone else's imagination, you fill that person with who you really are, it's the real you, in a mask, but it's the real you underneath. Does that make sense? I know I'm drunk, but I'm not talking out of my ass Bill."

"Yeah, I'm not drunk either. I think I understand you. Acting liberates you."

"Oh fuck yeah!" Woody turned around and waved his arm in the air. "Bill, exactly, are you a financial analyst Bill?"

"No, no I'm not."

"Are you Bill, Bill?"

"No, no I'm not."

"Are you free Bill?"

"Yeah, yeah, I'm free."

I felt like I had grabbed my moment of glory with Woody, his entourage seemed to be getting restless.

"I'll see you around Woody, and I'll make sure to watch more of your movies."

"Alright Bill, and I'll make sure to – be free Bill!"

When I went back to my hotel, I was out of my body. Who was I? Was I really that nobody living in a weekly motel in Reno? Was I this dude staying at the Grand Hyatt having one-night-stands, eating caviar, doing blow off $500 escorts, chatting with Woody Harrelson at exclusive night clubs? What the fuck was going on? Was I dreaming? One particular night after heavy drinking and snorting, I came home, stumbling about. I was in my underwear, and I looked at myself in the mirror. I went right up to my face. I didn't know who I was. I mean, I didn't recognize the face. It was just like this strange guy looking back at me. I'm not Bill. Who is Bill? Who am I really? It freaked me out, but I kept staring. It freaked me out more. I looked away. I said to myself, "That was just too fucking weird."

I actually really did want to find a girlfriend in New York and maybe even move there. I even considered Caroline, but that was pure insanity. It was all ecstatic fun and wild, but I always felt there was something missing. But on my sixth trip, it wasn't wonderland anymore. The novelty had died off. There were diminishing returns. Of course, looking back, the sixth trip, the seventh, the eighth were a fuck of a lot better than anything else I ever did since, and I'd kill to relive that sixth, seventh, eighth trip, and I probably have been chasing that high ever since, both the coke high and the high of self-indulgent, wealthy, luxuriant, sex with hot women life. There will never be anything like it ever again. How can I live with such an idea?

Back in Reno, Sean got rid of the data entry department. We were basically double-entering the data the customer service clerks were receiving, and now with online ordering, there was no need for us at all. But he just made me a 'Management Analyst' and kept me around, and I was traveling half the time. I'm not sure why. Maybe he just felt sorry for me, or maybe I was just a handy tool to inflate expenses and justify the shitload of money that was coming into eGo. Maybe he needed a mole in the ranks. Maybe that's what rich people do for poor people. Shit, you do a favor for someone and next thing you know, they put you on the board of RJ Reynolds or Philip Morris. I didn't know what to do with all the money. I blew a lot of it on escorts and coke. I often wondered if I had sold out to the devil, but Sean was right. I was only hurting myself by not playing the game. I used to be a fucking poor, sore loser.

Since I was on salary, I just had to check into the office a couple hours a day. I spent most of my time just socializing with everyone. I'm not sure anyone had any idea what I did. Sean promoted me to Senior Management Analyst. I was helping Sean with reports, investment analyses, finances, purchases. I actually helped Sean out with some spreadsheets and reports, but it took little time and I could usually pawn off most of the work on the other analysts who didn't have much work to do anyway. I figured they could get rid of a hundred people and still do the same amount of work, myself included. Maybe that's what happens during economic booms, everyone's employed, they're just not doing shit. So long as I was in with Sean, nobody questioned me. We didn't hang out as much as in the past, and I sort of missed being in that close circle, but there was enough partying and fucking to keep me busy. I even went out with two, young coworkers and fucked one. In hindsight, it was a great time, but of course, when you're in the moment, you're just concentrating on the next party, the next fuck.

One day, Terri in sales warned me of the stock bubble. He told me there was no way to justify the price earnings ratios. I didn't know what the hell he was talking about. He said the entire stock market was out of whack, and I should diversify and buy real estate. I had $250 thousand dollars in stock when eGo hit $50. I had bought more and more stocks along the way. I was considering taking out loans to buy more stock. If the stock hit $200, I'd be a fucking millionaire. There were smaller companies trading at $100 a share. Everyone was nuts. Of course, it is all hindsight now. It was irrational exuberance. I was high off coke too. Terri, however, was an old fuck from a bygone era. He had his heyday. He used to be a millionaire, but then something happened and he lost it all. Now he was a sales guy making $50K a year plus commission. He didn't know what the fuck he was talking about. There was no going back. The Internet was the future. It was like the railroads or automobile or computers. If you didn't jump in now, you'd be forever playing catch up.

You could balk at paying $100 a share now, and down the road when it hits $1000 a share, you'd be sorry.

I told Sean what Terri had told me, and the next day Terri was fired. Terri was a good man. He gave me a ride to San Francisco. I often look back on that with horror. I had sold my soul to Sean. I was Sean's stooge, his mole. Besides banging Marla, I regretted selling Terri out the most.

Having no clue that I had betrayed him, Terri invited me over to Midtowne Market. Or maybe Terri did know and was going to confront me or shoot me. I had no idea, but I was intrigued so I went over.

"Bill, good to see you. Did you see my new SUV out front?"

"Oh, that's yours? When did you get it?"

"Well, after I was let go, I cashed out my eGo shares and part of it went to that thing. I'm actually going give it to Heather to drive."

"Heather?"

"Yeah, Heather, you know the customer service clerk."

"The blonde? That Heather?"

"Yeah."

"You guys are going out?"

"Yeah."

"Jesus Christ Terri, you're old enough to be her dad, and you're married."

"Well, we're in the process of getting divorced."

"Then what? Are you going to marry Heather?" My mind was reeling. I would give my left nut to screw Heather. I was a little suspicious of the two of them, but never in my wildest dreams could I ever imagine a woman as young and attractive as her going out with this old, unattractive dude. Maybe she was using him as a sugar daddy? Hell, he was giving her a brand new SUV.

"Oh no, no. We'll just go out for a while, see what happens."

"Man, Terri, you the man."

"She's actually a very sweet kid. She was having a really hard time with her boyfriend, so I let her move into an apartment I set up for us until I got through my divorce."

"You've been living with her?"

"Oh yeah. Yeah, she walks around the place with these amazing see-through nighties, I mean Jesus Bill. Well, we're getting sidetracked."

Oh you fucking old dog I was saying to myself. You fucking lucky old dog. Jesus. I was paying $500 to bag a Russian hooker, and he was getting her for free, well, that is until the SUV.

"Are you giving her the SUV?"

"No, it's still under my name. She just needs a more reliable car. If things don't work out, I'll take it back. But the reason I called you out here Bill is that I got a job offer with Goldman Sachs selling bonds. Now, we all know the economy is going to crash soon, and NASDAQ, Dow, stocks all over the chart are going to get wiped out. But people are still going to be working, and they're still going to be paying into retirement and pension funds. There's still going to be institutional money to invest. Insurance companies, government, unions, they're all still going to want safe investments. The market will be bonds, and my friend at Goldman is telling me, they're creating exciting new bonds that will yield similar returns as stocks using derivatives, hedges."

"Well, I think that's great Terri, so you're going to New York?"

I was still trying to wrap my mind around him and Heather. That just mad me mad with envy.

"Yes, but we're going to need help. We need someone highly educated, analytical, smart, someone who can adapt quickly, work long hours, someone trustworthy. These are new, complex funding mechanisms, what they call Collateralized Debt Obligations. We need people to do the math, create the formulas, create the products."

"Okay."

"Someone like you Bill."

"Oh."

"Bill, the first day I met you, I had questions about you. You're a Stanford grad, but you've been doing data entry at $8/day for four years since you graduated. Why? I know the economy was tough back then in California, but where are your contacts? Where are your friends? Why not an entry-level job with opportunity instead, a data entry job is a dead-end. The only possible way up is as supervisor or data entry department manager, but even that's a dead end. How many data entry department managers ever became Vice Presidents and Presidents of the firm?"

"Okay, I see your point."

"But I saw something in you I didn't see in others. I saw hunger, and I was watching you as we grew, and I saw you become supervisor then department head and now management analyst. I saw the way Sean took a liking to you and promoted you and helped you out. Of all the people in the office, you knew how it all worked before anyone else. You knew the players, you knew how to get through, I saw how you worked with Marla and Sean. You see, I was blindsided at eGo. I thought I had it going well with Sean and Sam, even Marla. But I made my mistake. I didn't know anyone on the inside. I wish I had known you better. Maybe you know what happened? Who told Sean I was a problem, why, what was their benefit? Was it one of the junior sales guys? Did he want my position?"

I changed the subject.

"Terri, I'm not sure. I have a great job right now."

"Bill, like I told you, this bubble is not infinite. There is insufficient new capital to chase the over-inflated old capital. It has hit critical mass already. There are signs of the walls cracking. The P/E ratios are insane. You see it firsthand here. We're burning through cash faster than we know what to do with it. Have you seen our books? Our accountants have their heads up their asses. There are things we are buying that make no sense and prices that make no sense. There's a management analyst here who just got out of college making $100K a year and spends two months out of the year in New York doing who knows what? You ever noticed how everybody at the office had nothing to do except the janitor? It's unsustainable. The bubble is going to burst any moment. I am begging you Bill, sell your shares, join me at Goldman, sell derivatives and bonds, jump in early on the next big wave. Sell high and buy low. There is no better advice in investing. Jump on Goldman before the rest. Jump on the real estate market early and jump off the dot com boom right before it crashes."

Terri was a nutter, an old man who knew nothing about the future. Bonds were old school. Derivatives? Collateralized debt obligations? It all sounded like a load of BS. I wondered if Terri was going senile. This was only the middle of the dot com boom. We were only half way there. I figured I could probably sell in a couple years and retire for life. I didn't want to work the rest of my life. I didn't want to work for a big investment company crunching numbers at my desk 80 hours a week. Terri didn't know me enough. He didn't even know that I was the one who sold him out.

Midtowne Market was such a classy Sex and the City place. It stuck out like a sore thumb in Reno. You found places like this in Manhattan, but of course, the drinks would all be twice the price, and you wouldn't get college kids in jeans and t-shirts sitting at the bar. Reno was pathetic. Maybe I should have taken the Goldman Sachs job and moved to Manhattan. I always had wanted to move there. Maybe I could make enough to live in a decent one-bedroom apartment in Midtown instead of the studios I checked out in Chinatown. Maybe this was my ticket out of Reno? Maybe I should have given it more thought. Another fork in the road, but this time, I walked away.

At that moment Heather appeared.

"Oh, hey Heather."

Terri got up from his seat.

"You know Bill," he pointed to me as I waved.

"Yeah, Bill of course. How are you?"

"Good."

"So you got a secret for me?" she turned to Terri.

"Okay, babe, just a second. I'm finishing up a story with Bill. Tell you what, why don't you check out their wine list and find a Willamette Pinot Noir for dinner, and I'll come join you in a second."

"Okay," she smiled. They kissed on the lips. I thought I was going to be sick. Man, old hippie Terri was stilling getting babes.

"Look at that ass, isn't that something?"

I was beside myself with jealousy and envy. But then again, perhaps this only meant that when I turned 150, I could get some hot 20 year-old in the sack with me.

"Well, Bill, think about my proposal. Let me know. Get out of eGo before it's too late. Sell."

I shook his hand. I still could not believe he was going out with Heather. I was starting to think that Terri was a total loony bin, a lucky total loony bin. But if he was so wise and smart, he should never have hired me, because I was the one who betrayed him. Later Terri told me that Heather returned to her old boyfriend and tried to take his SUV until he had her arrested and got the vehicle back.

Chapter 11: Greed and Acedia

One evening, Sam grabbed me and took me out to the warehouse. Marla's death, his increasing irrelevance in the company, Sean, the stock market crash, he was losing his fucking mind.

"You hear that?"

I looked around puzzled. "Hear what?"

"That, that. That knocking. Over there, over there, that door." He pointed to the loading dock door.

I walked over closer. There was a little rattling of the door.

"It's probably the wind."

"No, no, no, it's not the wind." He slowly collapsed to the floor until he was on his back. His hands were over his eyes. "It's not. It's not. There's someone there. There's someone there. She's always there. She's out there."

I looked at Sam with shock. This dude was losing his fucking mind. I looked over at the door. I started to wonder myself if perhaps there was someone out there trying to fuck with his mind, trying to drive him nuts like in that movie *Deathtrap*. They were trying to fucking give him a heart attack and kill him. Maybe Sean wanted him dead and out of the picture.

He sat up. "Go over there. Go! Go look on the other side! Tell me what it is! Do it!"

"Maybe it's a dog or coyote. There's wild animals way out here."

"Then go find out! Go! Get out there!" He barked at me.

Jesus Christ, I said to myself and rolled my eyes. I called him right the first month in San Francisco that fucking nutbag.

As I approached the door next to the docking door, I got a tingling sensation up my neck. I was beginning to freak out. Maybe it was a ghost or some monster. What the fuck was out there?

I opened the door and stood halfway through it and looked at the other side of the docking door. The evenings were brighter now. No more going home in darkness. I could see everything out there. Fortunately, there was nothing there. I looked back over at Sam. He was on his back again. What a crazy fuck. I figured that he wouldn't be happy if I just took a peek and came back to him. I figured I could use some fresh air and a break from the crazy asshole, so I stuck a stone in the door to keep it open and looked to my left around the wall. Who knows, maybe I'd catch someone running down the side of the warehouse. I looked around trying to imagine what could possibly be hitting the docking door. Was it a bird flying into it? Was it wood from crates flying around and hitting it? Boxes? Garbage? I decided to go check the other end of the warehouse. Maybe I'd find a bunch of wild animals out there in the field.

I approached the corner of the building and looked out in the field. It had recovered a little from the fires, but I noticed something that stood out, a big clump that didn't look the same as the surroundings. I walked over toward it. As I got closer and closer, it started to take shape, and it wasn't just a heap of burned brush and debris. I came closer and closer, and then I realized what I was looking at. It was horrific. It was black. It had no fingers. It was a burned, decayed body. Jesus fucking Christ! It was a human corpse! I studied it for a moment. I was both sickened and fascinated by the details of beef jerky like strips of burned flesh, strands, interwoven, melted, torn, burned out. I thought to myself, maybe I shouldn't stare so long, I was basically searing it into my memory. It would never get out. I'd have nightmares. I'd never forget it. I turned away. I ran. I ran all the way back into the warehouse.

"Mr. Thompson! Mr. Thompson! Mr. Thompson!" I was screaming. I felt like a kid running to his mommy. "Mr. Thompson! There's a fucking dead body out there!"

Sam got off his back and looked at me. "Mom."

I didn't know whether to call 911 or the non-emergency line. It wasn't like someone was dying. I decided to call 911. A forensic team came out and put out yellow tape in a pretty large area around the body. I imagine there would be very little evidence; it was all burned and had been a while since the fires. I wondered if it might have been one of our workers who went out there during the forest fire, but nobody had gone missing except Marla. Shit.

A few weeks later, Sean came up to me in the break room. He told me that they had identified the body using the teeth. It was Marla.

There was a lot of talk in the office now that perhaps someone in the office had murdered Marla, and Sam was the obvious suspect. Sam was acting crazy recently, like he was losing his mind, and it was possible that it was from the guilt of killing someone, but the police seemed to remain focused on Tom. Why would he try to empty her checking account? It was too coincidental that a week after getting her to sell her eGo shares, she went missing, and he tried to get the money from the sale.

Several people in the office were called up to testify in front of a grand jury. I had no idea there was even was such a thing as a grand jury. Apparently, the DA presents his case in front of a grand jury before going to trial, and the grand jury determines if there's sufficient evidence to have a trial. I still felt that I was in shock. I was emotionally numb, flat, maybe it was all that coke.

I was surprised to see so many old folk on the grand jury. They must have bused them in from some retirement home. Maybe this is what happens when you retire, you sit on grand juries. Also surprisingly, the attorney from the DA's office was rather harsh on me. In hindsight, it was almost like a cross-examination. He threw a battery of questions at me. At first, it seemed innocent enough, like when did you first work with her, whom did she associate with, but then it just took this bizarre turn where he started throwing out weird questions.

"Why were you promoted to Assistant Manager and then Senior Management Analyst when you started as a data entry clerk?"

"Why did you get so many promotions and bonuses?"

"Why did you travel so much?"

"What are your qualifications as a Senior Management Analyst?"

I was asking myself, what the fuck does that have to do with anything? Was he trying to rattle me? Attack my ego? Make things personal? Get me to lose my temper and admit that I killed Marla? Was he going to go into my travel expenses and $3000 suits? He didn't even grill me about my relationship with Marla. This whole time, they had no idea that I had gone out with her a few times one-on-one and had a night where I made out with her and banged her. I thought the attorney was on my side. I wanted to share with the grand jury all the stories of Tom abusing her.

At the end, as the attorney escorted me to the door, I asked him if I could tell the grand jury about all that Marla had told me about what Tom did to her. He shook his head and led me out. I was confused.

I was later subpoenaed for the murder trial. It was my first and hopefully last. Right before the trial, the assistant DA brought us all into a conference room. There were cardboard boxes on some seats, and I asked him what were in the boxes, and he glibly replied, "Marla's remains." I was in shock. Was he kidding? What kind of joke was that if he was kidding? Did I just imagine him saying that? Did he in fact say that? I was tempted to open the boxes that were not even sealed, but I didn't. I could have had my Hamlet moment with the skull. I'm pretty sure he was kidding. What a sick fuck.

I was then called out and led to an area right outside the courtroom. I waited there a while before a guy came out and approached me. He had papers in his hands. He asked me if I recalled a statement I had made regarding some rumors that Marla had just recently met some guy who didn't work at eGo. I told him I remembered them, and he left.

I was called into the courtroom. I wasn't as nervous as before. I had already testified in front of a court, and this time, I felt more relaxed and confident. I remember reading or hearing somewhere that you're allowed to address the jury; and it's even a good idea if you want to connect with them and affirm your confidence and honesty.

The prosecutor asked me general questions again and then asked me to recount how I had come upon Marla's body. I didn't tell him the part about Sam going nuts thinking there was a ghost out there knocking on the warehouse door. I just told him that Sam heard a strange noise outside and wanted me to go investigate. I figured it was something hitting the warehouse door from the wind. I told the courtroom that I noticed something standing out in the distance and went over to investigate. I told them I had no idea it was Marla. People wondered why Tom would dump Marla's body behind the place she worked, but it made sense if he was trying to implicate someone working at eGo.

The defense attorney then came up, and he asked me if I recalled hearing something about a Scott Boylan, someone Marla had met soon before she disappeared. I told him I didn't remember that. He appeared stunned. I then realized it was the same guy who approached me outside. He wasn't with the prosecutor's office, he was with the defense. He didn't even identify himself.

"You don't recall having made a statement regarding Scott Boylan? Do you want me to read the statement you made regarding him?"

"Sure."

"Some of my coworkers told me that she had just met some guy named Scott, and they wondered if he might be involved."

"Oh. Well, that was just speculation. That was what one person said another person said about a rumor."

I caught the prosecutor smiling. The defense gave up on me. I had a mental fart. He must have thought I was deranged.

A few days later, Tom was convicted of murder. He received a life sentence.

Between March 20, 2000 to April 10, NASDAQ went from 4963 to 3321, a drop in value of one third. It was a warning to everyone, but we were all in denial. It was just an adjustment, we kept kidding ourselves. If I had sold then, I would have walked away with $250K, a quarter of a million. I refused to sell. But employees were selling, and eGo was dropping like a rock.

Every week, I could have sold. I could have walked away with $200k, $150K, $75K, $20K. I finally sold $10K worth of shares and left $10K. I split my odds. When it went down again, I sold the rest and walked away with $15K. I was dumbfounded. eGo's a penny stock now, garbage for bottom-feeding day traders. People were let go left and right, and I was counting my days. Oddly enough, it happened the day after I testified. I'll never forget the day. I put all my shit into a cardboard storage box. I threw away my collection of Burger King kid's meal toys. I drove my car down W 2nd Street when it went all the way out near Stoker. I drove downtown and drove south on Sierra. I was in shock. I was unemployed. My fortune was gone. The party was over, the traveling, the women, the coworkers, the camaraderie, all gone. It was devastating.

I couldn't work regularly for a couple years. I got hooked on coke for a bit. I had to give up my company car and soon wound up back on the bus system, back in a weekly motel. I went right through the $15K. I bought a lemon, traded it in for a new car but couldn't keep up with the payments. I could have gotten a job and used the $15K for a down payment on a house. Of course, there's no going back in time. eGo happened. What if I never got the job in the first place? What if I had never met Marla? What if I had never confronted Sean at Roxy's? I still remember that fork in the road, perhaps in a different universe I kept on walking to Brew Brothers. What if he never had taken me under his wing? What if I had never done coke, never learned to hit on women? What if I sold at $250K and bought a house in 2000? When the housing boom happened, I could have sold my $250K house for $550K in 2006. But then again, would I have sold in 2006 and netted $300K? I'd be worth over half a million bucks. What if, what if, what if. It's all just bullshit speculation.

I fell into a pit of despair, but I remembered what Sean had told me. I don't consider Sean to be a role model anymore. I started to idolize him, but with time, I realized he was just a human. He had his excesses and flaws. I ran into Mark who hooked up with an eGo coworker and stayed in Reno. He told me that Sean sold in April of 2000 and made millions. He moved to New York and then made millions more on the housing boom. Good for him. He got a seat at the table. He gave me Sean's number and told me I should call him. They lost my number when I couldn't afford my cell phone for a bit.

I'm glad I met Sean though, because he taught me about taking responsibility for my life and decisions, and either playing the game or standing on the sidelines heckling the players, it was my choice. I got my fair shot. I can't complain anymore. I make a decent salary now working at some government job. Maybe Sean was right. There are only a few seats at the wealthy table, but at least in America, everyone gets a shot at a seat, and we make our choices, play the game, and we should quit whining about players breaking the rules. It's not a fair game. It's not an ideal game. There are only so many winners, but I guess you can't have 99% winners.

"Bill?"

"Yeah, from eGo."

"Oh, right. Hey Bill. You in Reno?"

"Yeah, still here."

"Wow, great to hear from you. You ever finish up that novel of yours?"

"You know that's a funny thing. I ran into Mark, and I decided to write a new one about my experience at eGo."

"Ha!"

"Yeah, who knew right? Great material."

"Just change all the names right?"

"You know how it goes. Fiction. You mix and match. You take liberties. You add a little drama."

"You don't need to add any drama to that shit."

"Yeah, you're right."

We went through what had happened to each of us in the years between. I bullshitted. Hell, he could have been bullshitting. He was bragging about buying some 120 foot yacht and a time share in a Gulfstream jet. Whatever.

"You remember Marla?" I threw out there.

"Oh yeah, that crazy bitch. Yeah, I banged the fuck out of her."

"What? Really?"

"You didn't know that? I screwed her in my office, her office, in Sam's office, in the warehouse. No, she gave me a blow job while we were in Sam's office, and I was sitting on his chair. Oh yeah, and then we fucked on his desk." He laughed. "Shame what happened to her."

My suspicions were right. I remember Marla and Sean always staying late after work, Marla laughing loud, flirting, acting cheesy. I always thought she was fucking Sam, but maybe she was just fucking them both. I thought they were fooling around late at night, but I had no idea. When Sean told me, it just made it real, and my heart skipped a beat with jealousy.

It had just occurred to me that Sean and Sam were with Marla at the office the night of the fire, the last time outside of possibly her husband, that anyone saw her. It made me wonder what their stories were. Who was the last one to see Marla?

"So, there's just one thing I always wanted to ask you." I threw it out as if it was trivial in typical detective Columbo fashion as I was closing up the conversation.

"Sure."

"You remember that night of the forest fire."

"Yeah, crazy."

"We were like the last ones there. When I left, it was just you, Sam, and Marla right. You know who wound up the last one there?"

"Uh, I don't think so. When I left, it was Sam, Marla, and you. I saw your cars as I left."

"Really."

"Yeah. I was worried for you guys, but the fire department said the winds had changed, so we were okay for the night."

"Huh. Yeah it's been a while. No big deal. Well, cool. Hey, it was good talking to you again. I'm glad I got to know you. You taught me some pretty good things."

"Yeah, me too. I got to run Bill. You take care. Remember, don't stop playing the game."

"Right."

I sat there for a while. I tried to run that through my head again. I could have sworn Sean's car was there when I left. Was he bullshitting me? It was a black BMW M5. Sam had an older BMW 730i. I knew the difference between the two, and Marla had an older Nissan Maxima that looked like an older BMW 5 series. I kept trying to bring that picture back into my mind. I started to wonder why Sean was lying to me. Was he trying to make up some excuse that he wasn't the last one there? Why did he say that he saw my car there? Maybe he was just confused. Fuck, he probably did more blow than I ever did. Maybe I was confused.

I started to play out scenarios in my mind. Sam killing Marla after finding Sean and Marla fucking. Sean killing Marla perhaps accidentally after rough sex. Marla killing herself? Jumping off the warehouse roof? She was only about 20 feet from the warehouse. Sean was on the roof all night, he would have seen, or maybe he just watched, didn't really give a fuck if she jumped. Fuck me. I considered calling the police, reopening the case. I never told them that Marla was one of the last ones at the warehouse the night of the fire. They assumed she went home early like everyone else. I never told them that Sam or Sean were probably the last ones to see her before she went missing. What the fuck? Was I protecting Sean again? How much was my loyalty worth?

But then it occurred to me, Sean was saying it was me and Sam who saw her last. I could be implicated. I was a fucking suspect. Who would believe me? He'd hire some million dollar lawyer and turn everything around on me. I never called the police. I mean what if they went after me? What if they thought I killed her? That would just suck.

Made in United States
Troutdale, OR
10/04/2023

13416921R00087